The TREASURE of the LOST MINE

Gregory O. Smith

Also by Gregory O. Smith

The Wright Cousin Adventures

The Treasure of the Lost Mine

Desert Jeepers

The Secret of the Lost City

The Case of the Missing Princess

Secret Agents Don't Like Broccoli

The Great Submarine Adventure

Take to the Skies

The Wright Cousins Fly Again

Reach for the Stars

The Sword of Sutherlee

The Secret of Trifid Castle

The Clue in the Missing Plane

Additional Books

Rheebakken 2: Last Stand for Freedom

Strength of the Mountains

The Hat, George Washington, and Me!

"I can't believe it," declared Kimberly Wright. "Tim totally drew his spy guys on our brand-new book cover."

"What?" said Lindy.

"Hey, quiet girls," Jonathan said, "somebody's about to turn the page and read our book."

The TREASURE of the LOST MINE

Dedication

This book is dedicated to my patient and supportive wife and family, and to my 3 persevering editors—Lisa Smith, Anne Smith, and Dorothy Smith—without whom these books would not have been as legible or nearly as much fun!

Author's note

Many years ago, our family bought a small ranch up in the mountains. As we explored it, we found an old 1870 Gold Rush mine on the property. For more than a century, rain waters had washed dirt into the mine; we could barely crawl into it. We built a narrow-gauge railway to the mouth of the tunnel and began digging it out with pick and shovel. We used a "Truax Patented Automatic Dump Ore Car" built in 1898, to carry away the rock and debris a ton at a time. As we dug down, we found remnants of a 3-inch-thick wooden door at the mine's entrance, its rusty padlock still in place.

We were soon cleaning out the inside of the tunnel itself and were fascinated to see pick marks in the ceiling, walls, and floor made by the original miners. Inside the mine, we found many things left by the miners including a San Diego soda pop bottle from 1925.

We also rebuilt an old mining flat car we found in a shed on the property. The flat car had originally been used to haul an ore bucket full of rock by the previous miners, but our kids now used it for a "rollercoaster ride" out of the mine and down the hill. After several trips off the end of the track and into the canyon at the tailing pile, we discovered two more pressing needs on the railway: brakes and a new bridge.

Before we were done, we had acquired 7 historic battery-powered mining locomotives, built 22 passenger cars—including one for guests in wheelchairs—and laid over a mile of track. We were soon dressing up as Old West pioneers and giving train and gold mine tours to thousands of people from all around the world. Maybe you were one of the lucky ones who got to ride inside our old mine car you see on the book cover!

Getting out and experiencing the good things in life is totally fun, especially when you share it with family and friends!

That's why I started this book. When you join the Wright cousins, you'll get to dig into life; taste it, feel it, and make it yours! This is your chance! So grab your flashlight, hat, and tennis shoes and help the Wright cousins search for *THE TREASURE OF THE LOST MINE!*

~ Gregory O. Smith

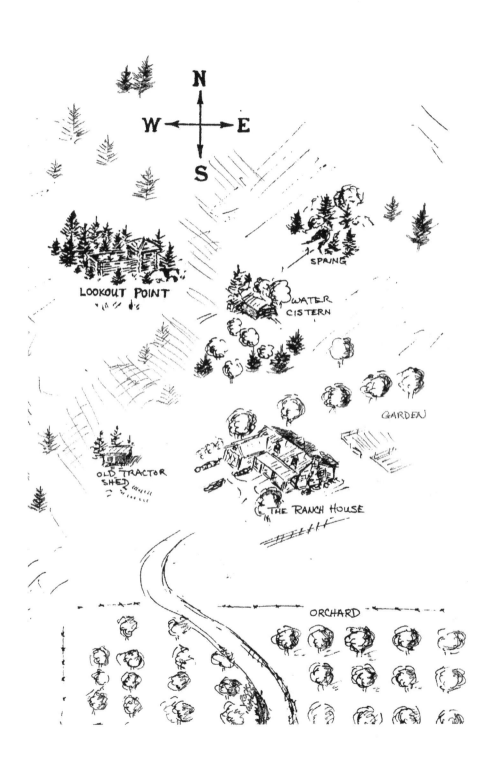

CHAPTER 1

Plane Trouble

Smoke blinded the pilot as he flicked the electronics kill-switch. The plane's gauges went dead. Flames licked the outside edges of the dash panel. Fumbling for his small fire extinguisher, he ripped it out of its rack and sprayed under the airplane's dash. The fire went out, but the cockpit filled with noxious, black-gray smoke. Gasping for breath, the pilot flung open his canopy to escape the fumes.

Sixteen-year-old Robert Wright, closing the front yard gate, watched in astonishment as the plane flew overhead and went down. He ran for the old Wright family ranch house and threw open the door. "Grandpa come quick!" he called out. "An airplane just crashed into the orchard!"

"What?" said white-haired Grandpa Wright, quickly rising

from his desk. Show me where. We'll take my pickup."

The five Wright cousins—twins Robert and Lindy and their three cousins, Jonathan, Kimberly, and Tim—had only arrived at the ranch an hour before and already there was trouble.

"Grandpa, can we come too?" Lindy called out. "We want to help."

"Then hurry and get in," said Grandpa as he fired up the pickup and the five Wright cousins climbed aboard. Grandpa didn't have to ask where the plane was; there was already smoke rising from the far side of the orchard. Bouncing on the gravelly road, Grandpa sped through the orchard and out the other side. They could see pieces of broken tree branches leading to a crumpled plane in the recently plowed field beyond. Black smoke was pouring from the plane's engine compartment.

Grandpa Wright jammed on his brakes and got out of the truck seventy-five yards from the crash. "You kids stay here. And call 9-1-1," he directed, and ran for the plane. Amidst the smoke pouring out of the cockpit, he could see the unconscious pilot slumped over. Reaching the plane, Grandpa tried to pull the pilot out, but the pilot was still strapped in and the smoke was getting more intense.

"Jonathan, bring your knife and help me get this pilot out!" Grandpa Wright shouted. "The rest of you kids stay back!"

Seventeen-year-old Jonathan Wright, the oldest and tallest of the Wright cousins, sprinted over to the plane.

"Cut the harness straps," said Grandpa Wright. "The buckles are jammed."

Taking a deep breath of clear air, Jonathan leaned into the cockpit and started cutting a strap. Black, acrid smoke burned his eyes. He finished the strap and went for another. He had to pull his head back out of the smoke, take another deep breath, and then start again on the second strap. His dull knife made the cutting more difficult.

"Who is he?" Jonathan gasped, finally done and pulling back again for fresh air.

"Jeb Carter," Grandpa said. "A good friend of mine. Let's grab him under the arms and get him out of here before the fuel explodes."

The smoke choked them as they pulled the unconscious pilot up and out of the cockpit. It was difficult to lift the man's full weight but they finally got him clear of the plane. Jonathan pulled the pilot up onto his back and carried him, heading for the truck. Grandpa was close behind. A hissing sound shrieked from the plane.

"Hit the dirt!" shouted Grandpa. They dropped to the ground.

With a thunderous *BOOM!* the aircraft exploded into a ball of flame.

Startled by the noise, the injured pilot began to stir. "My plane," he mumbled. "How could...my plane...I just had it worked on yesterday."

As the flames decreased, Grandpa and Jonathan got back to their feet and carried the pilot the remainder of the way to the pickup. Once there, they carefully set Jeb Carter down in the front passenger seat.

"Jeb, it's Charlie, where do you hurt?" asked Grandpa.

"I don't know," Jeb replied, stunned and staring at the burning wreck. "My plane is gone."

"Let it go, Jeb," said Grandpa Wright, trying to comfort the pilot. "Planes can be replaced, people can't. And if I know Jeb Carter like I think I do, you'll have a new plane and be back into organic crop-dusting in no time at all. You've always got my business."

"Thanks, Charlie," Jeb nodded. "Thanks for saving my life."

That's the kind of person Grandpa Charlie Wright was. He believed in helping people. He believed in working hard.

Grandpa could work men half his age into the ground. Because of poor crop prices, Grandpa had had to lay-off his hired hands and work the ranch alone. If Grandpa and Grandma couldn't turn things around soon, they would lose their ranch to government taxes.

That's where the five Wright cousins fit in. Their visit to their grandparents' ranch in the mountains had been planned for over a month. The idea had come up during a family council. When the cousins learned about their grandparents' predicament, they decided they really wanted to help them. Visiting the ranch always meant homemade ice cream and horseback riding through the mountains, but this time, it was also going to mean a lot of hard work. They would be the "hired" hands for a few weeks to help their grandparents save their ranch.

"Kids," said Grandpa, "I'm going to take Jeb to the doctor's in town. Grab the shovels from the back of the truck so you can keep that plane's fire from spreading. Put out the fire with dirt where you need to but keep your distance. I'll be back as soon as I can."

The cousins retrieved the shovels and headed for the burning plane. When they arrived, they could see pools of melted aluminum on the ground.

"Boy, what a mess," said Robert. "That plane will never fly again."

"What do you think happened?" asked Kimberly.

"It crashed," fourteen-year-old Tim said matter-of-factly.

"Thank you, *Tim*," said Kimberly, looking skyward. "*Brothers!*"

That afternoon, Grandma and the cousins got word about Jeb. He had several bad bruises but no broken bones. He was going to be okay.

There was a second reason the cousins wanted to visit the

ranch. It would give them a chance to do something they had been trying to do for a very long time. They wanted to find their great-great-Grandpa Jake's lost gold mine. And with their grandparents' financial challenges, it was this summer or *never*.

"Grandpa," said Jonathan at dinner that night, "we cousins have been talking. In our spare time, we want to help find the lost gold mine. It must still have some gold in it. Could you please refresh us on the clues he left?"

"Sure," began Grandpa, glancing at Grandma and then back to the eagerly listening cousins. "My Grandpa Jake was a pioneer. When he was young, during the 1800s, he married a girl from Tennessee. They moved out here to these mountains under homestead law. They built a log cabin and worked hard to make a good life for themselves. Over the years, they were blessed with five children. My dad was their youngest son. Grandpa Jake discovered gold on their ranch. The gold vein was rich enough that he was able to hire several men to help him in the mine. They were getting some pretty good color before the trouble."

"Color?" asked Tim.

"That means *gold*," said Robert.

"Oh, I knew that," said Tim.

"What kind of trouble?" asked Kimberly.

"One day, Grandpa Jake spied a rider comin' lickety-split towards his cabin. It was his brother, Bill, who brought word that a gang of bandits had attacked some settlers down the way and were wreaking havoc.

"'Jake,' he said, 'the bandits found out about your gold mine and they're gunning for you. If you won't tell them where it is, they're going to torture it out of you!'

Bill rode on to warn their sister's family in the next settlement.

"Grandpa Jake alerted his hired hands and neighbors and

they all evacuated their families to the old fort blockhouse up at Lookout Point.

"Sure enough, the bandits attacked the fort. The settlers defended themselves as best they could but were running low on bullets. Grandpa Jake went for more ammunition and was shot in the shoulder by one of the bandits as he was bringing it back up to the fort.

"The bandits were using a log, trying to batter in the fort's front gate. It meant certain death for all inside. Just as the gate gave way, the pioneers and bandits heard a distant bugle call."

"A bugle?" said Tim. "That means cavalry, right?"

Grandpa nodded. "The bugle call sounded again," he continued. "The bandits abandoned their attack and fled down the mountain in terror to save their miserable hides. But the cavalry never showed up."

"They didn't?" said Tim. "Then who sounded the bugle?"

"Nobody knows," said Grandpa. "But it signaled the end of the bandit trouble. Grandpa Jake and his family and the other folks returned to their homes only to find them burned to the ground. The bandits had been thorough. Everything would have to be rebuilt, but Grandpa and the settlers were grateful to be alive."

"What about the gold mine?" asked Tim.

"I was getting to that," said Grandpa Charlie Wright with a patient grin. "Grandpa Jake didn't want word getting out any more about his gold mine, so after the last of his hired help moved on, Grandpa Jake hid his mine and worked it on his own. He later left only a single clue about its location."

Grandpa paused for a moment as he retrieved an old, leather-bound book from a nearby bookcase. He returned to the cousins and said, "'Charlie,' he told me just before he died, 'the clue is in this book. If you find the mine, make sure the gold is only used for good purposes. And be careful...too much gold and idle time can sorely wreck a man.'"

CHAPTER 2

Clue in the Book

"What was the clue?" asked Robert.

"I'll show you," said Grandpa Charlie, opening the old book entitled *Farm Methods and Equipment.* "Now don't get your hopes up too high," he said. "I've looked it over from cover to cover over the last sixty years. The only peculiar part I could find was this handwritten note on the inside cover:

"Water problems 7/11/15—Page 49"

"Then the clue must be on page 49," said Tim excitedly. "Go there!"

Grandpa thumbed through the pages. "Let's see, page 49," he said, reaching the page and reading aloud, "Apple vinegar can be used to clean rust off of iron implements and machinery springs. First, fill a can with vinegar, placing the rusty tools in it to let them soak overnight. The longer the tool is left in the vinegar, the more rust will be removed."

The page went on to tell how important it was to always keep iron tools clean and properly oiled.

"That's a clue?" said Tim.

"Grandpa?" asked Lindy thoughtfully. "Did Grandpa Jake ever keep a journal? Maybe the clue is in it under the date 7/11/15, which would be July 11, 1915."

"If he had a journal, I've never been able to find it," replied Grandpa.

"Maybe 'water problems' means there was a flashflood that day," said Tim.

"Or maybe their well went dry," Kimberly said.

"They wouldn't need a well around here," said Lindy. "There's spring water flowing right out of the ground up on the side of the hill."

"To tell you the truth," Grandpa replied, "I thought of a flashflood, too. They're not too uncommon around here. When I researched it, the only thing I found was that in April of 1915, the old logging railway bridge was washed out during Spring flooding."

"Hmm," said Jonathan. "Water problems, a washed-out bridge, rusty tools. This is going to take some doing."

"Not tonight," said Grandma, interrupting their discussion. "It's time for all you ranch hands to hit the hay. We've got a big day ahead of us."

The next morning, Grandpa rousted the cousins out at 6 o'clock sharp. "Up and at 'em!" he called into the doorways of the boys' and girls' rooms. "We've got a lot of work to do."

After a quick, nourishing breakfast of toast, bacon, eggs, and fruit, Grandpa gave each cousin a brand-new pair of leather work gloves and assigned them to their tasks.

The sun was now up, and the day was already growing warm.

"Why does Grandpa's orchard have so many weeds?" complained Tim as they hoed around the trees.

"To keep *you* out of trouble," replied Kimberly.

"Me, get into trouble?" said Tim, leaning on the handle of his hoe.

"Back to work, Tim," said Kimberly, shaking her head.

"By the sweat of thy face shalt thou eat bread," added

Jonathan, chopping away at the weeds.

"Yeah," said Kimberly, elbowing Tim. "So, if you want to eat, you'd better get back to work."

"I'm working, I'm working," said Tim, starting to work again.

After finishing in the orchard, the Wright cousins helped Grandma in the berry patch. There were weeds to be pulled and berry plants to mulch with wood chips.

"Now this part's fun," said Grandma, pulling off her gloves. "Just dig your bare hands into the cedar chips. Grab big handfuls and pack the chips gently under each berry plant. The chips smell so good, you won't mind getting them all over your hands."

Next came the watering. The cousins talked as they worked.

"Maybe Grandpa Jake's lost gold mine was part of the *Glory-Be Mine*," said Jonathan. "Remember, we wanted to go there last summer but never got the chance. It's just upstream from the bridge that washed out in 1915. Maybe we should explore there first."

After finishing the berry patch, the cousins got permission to go exploring.

"Just be careful," admonished Grandma, "I don't want any of you kids getting hurt. And watch out for ticks and snakes, they're really bad this year."

The cousins first started exploring by computer at the ranch house. After some searching of old maps, they finally located the *Glory-Be Mine*. It had been abandoned for many decades. They found that it was okay to go hiking there as it wasn't on private land. They also noted there were two ways to get to the mine from their grandparents' ranch. The first was the roundabout way through their grandparents' orchards to the point of the mountain, then turn north past the washed-out bridge, and follow the abandoned railway tracks leading north through Coldwater Canyon.

The second way to the *Glory-Be Mine* was a more direct, but rugged route. It involved hiking northwest up to Lookout Point, on their grandparents' property, and down the other side of the mountain to Coldwater Canyon. Once in the canyon, they could follow the railroad tracks north to the Glory-Be Mine.

After a quick huddle, the cousins decided to take the more direct route through Lookout Point. That way they could "kill two birds with one stone": they could check out the old log fort and blockhouse ruins at Lookout Point and also explore the *Glory-be Mine*.

The cousins quickly rounded up canteens, food, broad-brimmed hats, and flashlights and started out. The thick brush of the uncleared mountainside made it more difficult than they had expected. Jonathan and Robert, leading the way, had to hack through the brush with machetes to blaze a trail for the others to follow. The cousins were hot, sweaty, and dusty by the time they finally arrived at the top of the ridge near Lookout Point.

"Where's the fort?" asked Tim, looking curiously at the small clearing around them.

"I think we're standing in it," said Jonathan, pointing toward a low pile of rotting logs surrounding them.

"This is a fort? But what happened to the blockhouse?" asked Tim.

"My guess is termites," said Robert.

"Those dirty rotten little buggers," said Tim. "So, where did the settlers have their cannon?"

"Grandpa didn't say anything about a cannon," Kimberly replied.

"Kimberly," said Tim. "A fort *has* to have a cannon, otherwise, well, it's just got to!"

The cousins explored the log fort site. Leaving no timber

unturned, they anxiously probed for clues that might help them. Jonathan discovered a rusty iron bar beneath one of the logs. It was stuck, so he gave it a hard tug. It didn't budge. "Tim and Robert," he said, "give me a hand with this."

Both boys came to help. "It looks like an old rifle barrel," said Tim eagerly.

"Could be," said Jonathan, resetting his grip on the steel bar. "All together on three. One. Two. Three!"

The three boys threw their combined weight against the bar. The bar suddenly broke free and so did the ground beneath their feet.

Out of the corner of her eye, Kimberly saw the earth swallow up the boys. Shrieking, she raced over to where the boys had just disappeared and skidded to a stop at the edge of a large chasm. Lindy joined her. Dust was billowing out. They couldn't see the boys or how deep the hole was. Lindy leaned forward to look.

"Careful," said Kimberly, putting her arm out to keep Lindy back. "It might be a mine shaft or something."

Lindy cautiously edged her way closer to the hole. "Robert, Jonathan, Tim," she called out, "are you guys okay?" She was answered by coughs and groans.

Lindy retrieved her flashlight and shined it down, hunting for the boys. As the dust cleared, she was relieved to see them piled up about ten feet below her on the floor of a small room. There was rubble underneath them.

"You boys okay?" Lindy asked with relief.

"Fine, just fine," Tim replied with a groan. "Nothing that a few weeks in the hospital won't cure. Somebody get these guys off of me. I'm squished!"

The two older boys slowly got to their feet and helped Tim up.

"Thanks for breaking our fall," said Jonathan. "At least you had your backpack to land on."

"My jelly-filled donuts!" Tim said in alarm. He quickly unzipped his backpack, reached in, and pulled one out. "Flat as a squished caterpillar," he said, shaking his head at the ooey-gooey mess. He took a bite. "But at least they still taste good."

"Gross, Tim," said Kimberly, peering over the top of the hole.

"Hey Lindy," said Robert. "Toss me down your flashlight." Catching the light, Robert shined it around. They were in the middle of a small, rock-lined room. A log bench ran along one of the walls. At the opposite end of the room lay a collapsed table.

Robert first checked the bench over and picked up one end.

"Watch out for rattlesnakes," called down Kimberly.

Robert immediately dropped the bench and stepped back. He studied it for a minute and picked the end up again. "Hey, what's this?" he said.

"What did you find?" Lindy called down.

"A leather pouch," informed Robert, dusting it off. "And it has something in it." The cousins were all eyes as Robert reached into the pouch and took out a black and green ball. "Aw, rats," he said. "It's just an old marble."

Lindy leaned down over the edge of the hole. "Let's see it." Robert tossed the marble up to her and she examined it more closely in the sunlight. "Feels too heavy to be a marble," she said. As she rubbed the dirt off the small object, a deep yellow luster caught her eye. "Wait a minute," she said excitedly. "This isn't a glass marble. It's made of *gold!*"

CHAPTER 3

The *Glory-Be Mine*

It was just getting dark as the cousins worked their way back down the mountainside from Lookout Point. They had searched the old fort from top to bottom but found nothing else of interest. Excited by their golden find, they never did make it to the *Glory-Be Mine* that day.

At the ranch house, the cousins eagerly told their grandparents about the secret room and the golden marble they had found.

"In all my years of looking," said Grandpa as he studied the golden ball and leather pouch under a magnifying glass, "I've certainly never found anything like this."

"Where do you think it came from," asked Tim.

"One of the old pioneers," Grandpa replied. "Probably cast it themselves so they wouldn't lose it as gold dust."

"Grandpa, what do you think the room was for?" asked Kimberly.

Grandpa thought for a moment and answered, "Maybe a powder bunker where they kept their gunpowder. Or, it could have been a safe room; kind of a last defense for the settlers to hide in if the enemy overran the blockhouse."

The next morning, the Wright cousins worked hard at their chores. They were eager to continue their hunt for the lost mine. Tim still had his moments of distraction, though. More than once, Kimberly caught him hanging upside-down in a fruit tree and had to persuade him to get back to work. The cousins finished their day's tasks by lunchtime and restocked their backpacks for their afternoon adventure.

"You kids be careful," Grandpa Charlie said. "Jonathan, you're the oldest. You're in charge. No owies. And if you see anything unusual, let me know."

"Got it," said Jonathan.

"Hear that, Tim?" said Kimberly. "No owies."

"Don't worry, sis, I've still got my jelly-filled donuts in here," said Tim, motioning toward his backpack.

"Oh, gross," said Kimberly.

"Don't worry, Kimberly," said Robert, "he's just teasing you. We actually finished them off last night."

Having already explored Lookout Point, the cousins gathered supplies and this time took the roundabout way to the mine.

"What do you think Grandpa meant about 'anything unusual'?" Tim asked as they walked, not sure whether he should get the heebie-jeebies or not.

"Oh, you know," said Kimberly. "Unusual things. Probably just monsters and things like that."

"Or Limburger cheese," added Robert.

"That smelly stuff? I'll take the monsters any day," Tim replied, and he ran to catch up with Jonathan.

When the cousins arrived at the old logging railway tracks, they turned north to follow the old train's path. Off to the west, in the distance, they could see the remains of the bridge across Coldwater Stream. Through binoculars, they could see steel girders, resting upon concrete pillars that rose from the water. The bridge was old and rusty and one-third of it was missing.

"I thought the whole bridge would be missing," said Jonathan.

"Me too," said Robert.

On the far bank, they could see the concrete ruins of the old 50-stamp mill. During the gold rush, the mill had been used to crush and process the ore from the gold mines further up the canyon.

"Hey, come on you guys, let's go," said Tim, stepping up onto one of the four-inch-tall rails they had been following. "Let's see who can walk the farthest on top of the railway track without falling off."

Putting away their binoculars, the cousins all tried walking on top of the rail. Balancing and staying on the rail was more challenging than they thought it would be. Kimberly set the record by walking two hundred steps before she finally slipped off the track onto the ground. The rails led them along the eastern side of the canyon, winding in and out of stands of pines and oaks. The railroad track was remarkably clear of brush and trees. After several miles, they came to a fork in the tracks.

"Grandpa said to take the left fork," remembered Lindy. "It leads closer to Coldwater Stream and the mine."

Unlike the main line they had been walking on, the new tracks were less used and were overgrown with weeds. The tracks led the cousins into a fragrant forest of tall, green cedar and pine trees. The area had been logged decades before, and the cousins could occasionally see the remnants of large stumps here and there. Pinecones and pine needles covered the ground. New-growth cedars and pines had filled in the area and long sections of the track were completely shaded by the beautiful trees. It made the cousins feel like they were travelling back in time.

As they rounded a curve, the cousins could hear the distant sound of rushing water. Soon the pine trees gave way to a lush, green meadow. At the far side of the clearing, they could see a rusty ore car still on the tracks.

"A mine car!" shouted Robert, breaking into a run and cutting across the meadow. "Last one there's a *rotten egg spaghetti juice noodle!*" he called out, and the race was on!

Well ahead of everyone else, Robert suddenly flung out his arms for balance as he tried to stop on the slick grass. Lindy and Jonathan caught him just as he was about to go over the edge and tumble down the steep slope into the rushing white water of Coldwater Stream.

"Thanks," said Robert, catching his breath. "I forgot about the river."

To Robert's right, the three-ton ore car, still on the tracks, was hanging precariously over the edge of the ravine. The twenty-five-foot long wooden trestle bridge it had been sitting on had been completely washed away by Coldwater Stream. Now, only two thin rails drooped across the void. Here and there, a weathered wooden railroad tie, still spiked in place, clung to the tracks. On the far side of the stream was the dark tunnel entrance to the *Glory-Be Mine*.

"So I'm confused," said Tim. "Is this the washed-out bridge Grandpa Charlie was talking about in 1915 or is it the other one?"

"Good question," Jonathan replied. "The answer to that probably lies in that mine over there. Let's figure out how we can get across this river."

Tim slid down the bank and stuck his hand into the water of Coldwater Stream. "Hey guys," he said, yanking it back out, "that water's *freezing!*"

"Aw Tim," said Jonathan, "you're just getting soft. Mountain water's great for you. You could give us piggyback rides."

"Not me," said Tim. "Robert's the scuba diver."

"It would take more than a wetsuit to get through that,"

Robert replied. "There's too much current."

Lindy had been eying the tracks and had an idea. "We could walk across," she said.

"Walk across?" said Tim. "Lindy, are you feeling okay?"

"No, I'm serious," Lindy continued. "We could balance-walk on the rails, like we were just doing, except with a foot on each rail this time for stability."

Jonathan studied the rails and splice bars. "The track looks like it would hold us," he said thoughtfully. "To lighten its load, we could pull the mine car back onto the solid ground and chock its wheels."

"Are you guys serious?" asked Kimberly. "Look at that rushing water!" The others nodded.

"Well," Kimberly said, taking a deep breath, "if we're going to try this, we'd better put up a rope safety railing or something. We'll have to have something to hold onto."

"Okay, Kimberly, what have you got for us?" asked Jonathan, knowing his sister kept a miniature supply of survival gear.

"Fifty-two feet of parachute cord," said Kimberly, "but it would kind of be too thin for a handle."

"I've got some rope in my backpack we can use," offered Robert.

"Okay," said Jonathan, "first, let's get the mine car secured."

The Wright cousins carefully pulled the mine car back from the edge of the stream bank to get its weight off the dangling tracks. It was old and rusty, but its greasy bearings were still good, and it did roll. They chocked the wheels with wooden sticks and rocks so it wouldn't roll back.

"Who wants to be the guinea pig—I mean—go first?" asked Robert.

Since it was her idea in the first place, Lindy agreed to go.

"Not without a safety rope," said Robert. He dug a rope out of his backpack, tied a knotted 'honda' loop into the end of it, and made a lariat. Making a large loop in the rope, he swung it above his head, cowboy style, and tried to lasso a large stump on the far side of the stream. After several attempts, he finally got it. He yanked on the rope to make sure it was securely anchored; the rope held. He tied the rope end which he was holding, onto a handle of the ore car next to him. The handrail rope was now secure.

Jonathan got out another rope from Robert's bag and they tied it around Lindy's waist as a safety line. Once that was done, Lindy stepped onto the dangling tracks.

"Be careful, Sis," Robert said encouragingly.

"Don't worry," Lindy said smiling back. "Safety's my middle name."

"I thought that was Kimberly's middle name," quipped Tim.

"Funny man," said Kimberly.

With the cousins holding onto Lindy's safety line, Lindy began to inch her way, one foot on each rail, across the old railroad tracks. The top of each rail was about one-and-a-half-inches wide and rusty, giving Lindy some traction. Part way across, she looked down at the clear, rushing water nine feet beneath her and froze.

"Don't look down!" yelled Robert. "Just keep going. Hold onto that handrail rope and keep moving. You'll make it just fine."

Lindy took a deep breath and started moving again. When she was within three feet of the opposite bank, she jumped and landed on the shore.

"Good job!" Robert called out. "Now, take your waist rope off and wrap it around that tree behind you. That way, we'll have two handrails, like on a rope bridge."

Lindy secured the rope and the rest of the Wright cousins, one at a time, began crossing the stream. Tim was the last to go. Halfway across, a leaping fish startled him. Tim flinched, slipped off the tracks, and plunged feetfirst into the river. The girls screamed. Tim was holding onto a single safety rope as he went underwater.

"Grab the rope!" shouted Jonathan.

The four cousins threw their weight into the line. The rope tightened. Tim's arms and head burst from the water. "Ai-yeeeeeeeee!" he said, squealing like a banshee. The cousins pulled harder, lifting Tim out of the water to his knees. The river's current was pulling at him.

"Hang on, Tim!" screamed Kimberly.

"Pull harder!" shouted Jonathan. The cousins pulled with all their might. Tim was finally free of the water. Shivering with cold, Tim worked his way hand-over-hand along the rope toward the other cousins.

"You can do it, Tim. Just a little further," Kimberly encouraged.

Still holding onto the rope, Jonathan reached out, grabbed hold of Tim's wrist, and swung him up onto the bank. He landed with a *thunk*.

"Good job, Timbo," said Jonathan, "but no more swimming with the fish, okay?"

"Okay," Tim shivered in reply. "Th-thanks for pulling me out."

The cousins had Tim sit on a large boulder and thaw out in the mid-day sun. When he was ready, they all walked over to investigate the *Glory-Be Mine*.

In its heyday, the *Glory-Be Mine* had been one of the biggest gold producers in the area. According to Grandpa Wright, nearly a hundred miners were employed there at one time, but the rich gold vein had suddenly pinched-out and the mine was shut down. Grandpa said the large mine had eight different levels of tunnels and over four miles of track. The ore from the mine had been hauled by railway to the large, specially built 50-

stamp mill downstream to be crushed.

The five cousins retrieved their flashlights and cautiously entered the mine. Inside, the air was cooler and slightly damp. On the right-hand side of the tracks, a rusty iron air pipe ran along the floor. The tunnel was about five feet wide and seven feet tall. Fifty feet in, they found their way blocked by a wall of rubble. The cousins shined their lights at the walls, ceiling, and floor.

"See those drill holes there in the rock," said Jonathan. "This isn't just a cave-in. Somebody's blasted this mine closed."

"Why?" asked Kimberly.

"To keep people out," said Jonathan.

"Hey, you guys," interrupted Tim, "did you notice that the ceiling is starting to move?"

Jonathan shined his light at the ceiling. It was covered with hundreds of brownish-black objects. The bright light made them start to move even more.

"Bats!" said Jonathan, shining his light away from them.

"Bats are good," said Kimberly.

"Not if they suck your blood," Tim replied. "Let's get out of here!"

"Timothy Wright, they do *not* suck your blood," said Kimberly.

"Oh yeah," said Tim, "then why are they starting to fly around us."

"They're looking for bugs," Kimberly said. "That's what they eat."

"Yeah, well I'm not a bug," said Tim.

"True," said Kimberly, "you're more of a pest."

"I am not a pest!" said Tim, grabbing up a handful of dirt and throwing it at Kimberly. Some of the dirt hit the ceiling of the tunnel and the bats *really* started moving.

"Let's get out of here," said Robert. "I haven't had my rabies shot."

"Me neither," said Tim.

The air was swarming with bats as the Wright cousins scrambled to get out of the old mine tunnel. Bats brushed the cousins' faces and necks as they ran.

The cousins burst from the mine and ran clear to the banks of Coldwater Stream. Many bats followed them. A writhing bat was stuck in Kimberly's hair. "Get it off me, get it off me!" she screamed frantically, trying to brush it off.

"Hold still," said Lindy as she tried to get the bat free. "It's only a little bat."

"I've heard of bats in your belfry," said Tim, "but this one takes the cake."

"Tim, don't joke like that," Lindy replied. "This poor little bat is scared to death!"

"The bat?" said Kimberly in surprise. "What about me?!"

"Oh, you're scared pretty good, too, Kimberly," said Tim.

When the bat was finally free from Kimberly's hair, it flew over to join the other bats swarming at the mine entrance. After several minutes, the dodging bats began to settle down.

The cousins washed their hands in the stream and decided to explore the mine a little more, on the *outside* this time. Robert and Tim found the remnants of an old waterwheel-powered air compressor. To the left the mine portal, Jonathan found parts of another old mine car; two of its wheels were missing. They also found an old electrical breaker box and some insulated wires for lighting, as well as a pile of rusty mine car track and some old drill steels for large pneumatic drills.

"Well, one thing's for sure," said Jonathan, "this isn't Grandpa Jake's mine."

"What makes you say that?" asked Kimberly.

"Well, for one thing," Jonathan replied, "the wiring, the pneumatic drills, this equipment is all too new. Jake would have used a pick and shovel to dig his mine. Also, Grandpa Jake hid his gold mine so it couldn't be found. This mine hasn't been hidden; it's just been closed."

While Jonathan was talking with the girls, Robert and Tim tried climbing up the mountainside to check out another possible opening to the mine. When they got to it, they found that it, too, had been blasted closed at the entrance. They were about to head back down the mountain when Robert said, "Did you hear that?"

"What?" said Tim.

"Listen," whispered Robert.

"You aren't trying to scare me, are you?" Tim asked suspiciously.

"Of course not," Robert replied. "Listen."

"I don't hear anything," said Tim.

Robert held a shushing finger to his lips. A moment later, both boys heard a soft thumping, screeching sound. "There it goes again," said Robert.

"What do you think it is?" asked Tim.

The sound seemed to be coming from somewhere up the canyon to the north. Robert caught glimpse of a large, black shape moving through the trees on the far side of the canyon. "What?" he said, rubbing his eyes in disbelief, "There haven't been any trains on those tracks for over a hundred years. What's going on?"

CHAPTER 4

Ghost Train

From their vantage point, Robert and Tim could see a black locomotive pulling four hopper cars loaded with grayish-tan rock. Tim got so excited he nearly fell off the mountain. "Hey, you guys," he shouted to the cousins down below. "There's a train over there!"

Robert and Tim quickly slid down the hillside to join the others. Robert pulled ahead. "There's a train," he announced excitedly, huffing and puffing, "We both saw it. It's running on the old logging tracks. If we hurry, we might be able to catch it and see where it's going."

"Grandpa didn't say anything about a train," said Jonathan. "Let's check it out."

The cousins quickly scrambled across Coldwater Stream, this time with Tim in the middle. Robert had rigged the lines so they could shake them loose from the mine car side of the stream. Once over, they retrieved their lines and stashed them in their backpacks.

"We'll never catch that train now," complained Tim.

"Oh yeah?" said Robert. "We can if we use this old mine car."

"Good idea," said Jonathan. "Kimberly and Lindy, you climb in the mine car with our gear. We'll join you as soon as we get it rolling fast enough."

After removing the sticks and rocks that blocked the mine car's wheels, the boys began pushing it down the track. It was hard at first, but soon it was starting to roll on its own. The car's wheels made a loud rumbling sound as it began picking up speed. At the last moment, the three boys jumped onto the car and climbed in.

"Robert are you sure you know how to drive this thing?" asked Kimberly as the mine car sped down the tracks.

"What's there to know?" said Robert. "We just sit back and let the railroad tracks do the steering."

"But what about the brakes?" shouted Lindy over the rumble of the mine car.

"*What* brakes?" said Robert. "Oops."

Jonathan winced. "I think we might have a problem."

"Pine tree ahead," warned Lindy. "Everybody duck!"

The mine car plowed through the pine tree branches and kept on going.

"That wasn't a duck," called out Tim. They were now going fast enough to fly a kite.

"There's a sharp curve ahead," shouted Jonathan. "Everybody lean to the right!"

Riding in the car was beginning to feel like a rollercoaster ride. The mine car hit the curve, clinging to the tracks. It plowed through a safety-type switch and merged onto the main logging railroad tracks. The cousins could see the mysterious train a half a mile ahead.

"Do you think we can catch it?" hollered Tim.

"With this downgrade we might," Robert called back.

"But what if we do catch it and run into it?" asked Kimberly. "That would be dangerous."

"I saw a movie once where these guys were chasing a train and they were about to hit it," said Tim.

"What did they do?" asked Kimberly.

"They jumped," Tim said.

"Were they okay?" asked Kimberly.

"I don't know, they were on a really tall bridge," said Tim.

"Speaking of bridges," Kimberly hollered, "aren't we getting close to that washed-out bridge at the 50-stamp mill?"

"Yeah," said Lindy, "why isn't that train slowing down?"

Entering an area of thick trees, the cousins lost sight of the train for about ninety seconds as they wove through the final curves before the mill bridge. They expected to hear a terrible crash at any moment.

Breaking into the open again, the cousins' mine car roared straight toward the broken bridge.

"Where's the train?" asked Robert in surprise.

"I don't know," replied Jonathan, "but it's time to go. Everybody *BAIL OUT!*"

The Wright cousins climbed over the sides and leapt from their speeding mine car. They went tumbling head-over-heels through the deep meadow grass before finally coming to a stop. Their mine car shot off the incomplete bridge and plunged into Coldwater Stream with a large splash.

"Everybody okay?" called out Jonathan from the tall grass he had landed in.

"I'm okay," Robert called back.

"Same here," reported Lindy. "Just have grass stains all over my nice jeans."

"Me too," added Kimberly. "Timothy, where are you?"

"Over here," Tim replied dizzily. "I think I lost a shoe. No, wait, I found it. It's in my back pocket. That's crazy."

The rest of the cousins soon gathered. Tim was trying to make it over to them, but he was so dizzy that he kept walking around in circles. He finally gave up and collapsed in the deep meadow grass, mumbling something about "bats and termites and rolleycoaster rides."

Once Tim had joined them, the cousins made their way over to Coldwater Stream to try to locate their mine car and the mysterious train. Walking out to the missing section of the bridge, they could see their mine car near the next bridge pilings under several feet of water. The train they had followed was nowhere to be seen.

"Where'd the train go?" asked Tim.

"I can just see it now," said Robert. "When we tell Grandpa about this. 'Guess what, Grandpa Charlie, we found an old train today.' 'Really?' he'll say. 'Yes, it was running on the old logging tracks. We followed it, but it kind of disappeared.'"

"Not just kind of, it *did* disappear," input Lindy.

"Grandpa's going to think we're cuckoo or something," said Robert. "And then we'll lose our exploring privileges and we'll have to hoe weeds for the rest of the summer."

"Maybe it was just a pigment of our imagination," suggested Tim.

"That's *figment*," corrected Kimberly.

"Then we all must have the same imagination," said Lindy, "because we all just finished chasing a ghost train down these tracks."

"That's it!" said Tim. "It *was* a ghost train, but instead of saying 'Boo!' it said, 'Choo!' Get it guys? Choo-choo. That's why it could disappear. It was a ghost train."

"Tim, that doesn't make any sense at all," said Kimberly.

"All in favor of us helping Tim take another swim in Coldwater Stream," teased Jonathan, "raise your hand."

Everyone raised their hand except Tim.

Jonathan looked down into the rushing stream and back at the tracks. The sun reflected brightly off the two, rusty rails. Then he realized what he was looking at. "Hey, wait a minute," he said to the others, "these tracks have been used a lot lately. See how the sides of the rails are rusty, but the tops are all shiny?"

CHAPTER 5

The Old Tractor

"Shiny?" said Kimberly. "Would the mine car we just rode on make the rails shiny like that?"

"No," Jonathan replied, "it just rolled across them once. It barely scratched the surface. It would have to go back and forth on it a whole bunch of times to get all that rust worn off."

"That does it," said Tim. "The ghost train is real!"

That evening, when the cousins told Grandpa about their adventures of the day, he was very concerned. "I don't like this idea of a ghost train," he said. "Sounds like somebody's up to no good." Perhaps there *was* some truth to the rumors he'd heard around town lately.

The next morning, Grandpa assigned the cousins their chores for the day and left soon afterwards.

"Grandma, where's Grandpa going today?" asked Kimberly at breakfast, sensing a tenseness in the air.

"He's got to go down to the county planning offices to get some new permits," answered Grandma matter-of-factly.

The cousins worked hard all day, irrigating crops and also pulling weeds in the orchard. Grandpa didn't arrive home until well after dark. The cousins were in the next room washing up for dinner and couldn't help but overhear their grandparents' conversation.

"Hi sweetheart, was it as bad as you thought it would be?"

the cousins heard their grandmother ask.

"Worse," said Grandpa. "We have 30 days to pay for their permits or they'll shut us down. It's bad, Honey. They want $2,000 for each time we use our tractor to plow our fields. Storing our grain in silos is another $1,500. We have to have a permit to do everything now. We can't even build a fence or plant a tree without a county permit!"

"That's ridiculous," said Grandma. "They can't do that to us small farmers. We don't make that much money."

"*They're* doing it," Grandpa replied. "I believe in good government, but this *isn't* good government. They're stealing our hard-earned money. We'll probably have to sell our new tractor just to pay the permit fees. We grow fruit, raise beef cattle, and have beehives to provide food for people all around the world. Does the county really want to destroy that?"

"Okay, this is bad!" said Grandma. "We've got to talk with our fellow farmers this week and fight this together. This is "taxation without representation" in the name of "permit fees." We'll probably have to pool our money to hire a land use attorney. We have to take action."

"We're going to take action, too," whispered Jonathan to the other cousins in the next room. "We can't let the county steal Grandma and Grandpa's land. We're going to work harder and smarter around here."

"And find Grandpa Jake's mine," added Robert.

"Yeah," said Tim.

When the cousins came in for lunch the next day, they found their grandpa talking with a dark-haired man in the living room. The man appeared to be in his early fifties.

"Kids," introduced Grandpa. "This is Juan Martinez. He's a good friend of mine and owns a ranch down the road."

The cousins shook hands with Mr. Juan Martinez, chatted for a moment, and then excused themselves to go get lunch.

"Growing kids are always hungry," said Mr. Martinez with a smile. "You should see how much my sons eat when they're home from college!"

While they were making their sandwiches in the kitchen, the cousins couldn't help overhearing Grandpa and Mr. Martinez's conversation.

"Something's going on," said Mr. Martinez. "I've never had thistle plants in my fields before, but now, all of a sudden, my fields are full of those horrible weeds. And did you hear? The county has now declared that thistle, black widow spiders, and rattlesnakes are all endangered species!"

"Something fishy *is* going on around here," Robert whispered to the other cousins, "and it's not just my tuna sandwich!"

That afternoon, the girls and Tim helped Grandma paint the outside of the chicken house with a fresh coat of "barn red" paint. Meanwhile, Jonathan and Robert donned their mechanics clothes and headed to the barn to help Grandpa try to bring his *old* tractor back to life.

"After all these years, we finally saved up enough money to pay cash for a new tractor," complained Grandpa Charlie, "and then we have to sell it before the season is even over." He looked at Jonathan and Robert and back at the tired old vehicle. "Well, we may as well get started."

Robert climbed up onto the front of the old tractor. "Why don't you just buy a new one on credit?"

"It costs a whole lot more money to buy things on credit, son, because of all the interest fees they make you pay," replied Grandpa as he inspected the air cleaner. "*Those who understand interest, earn it. Those who don't, pay it.* Well, let's see if we can get this old bucket of bolts running again. Here, put on some of these nitrile gloves and safety glasses, and we'll get to work."

Grandpa Charlie started checking the electrical system,

including the starter, while Robert and Jonathan started working on the fuel system.

"Hey Robert, hand me that socket wrench over there," said Jonathan, motioning toward the toolbox. Jonathan snugged down a bolt on the old 1940s carburetor and said admiringly, "They sure don't make them like this anymore."

"They sure don't," replied Grandpa. "This is the most mule-headed piece of machinery I've ever owned!"

"Robert, try working the throttle now," directed Jonathan.

Robert climbed into the old tractor and worked the gas pedal up and down with his foot.

"Okay, I think that's fixed," said Jonathan.

Still in the driver's seat, Robert cleaned the dusty cobwebs off the old gauges on the dash. He tried the horn switch; it squeaked for a second and went dead. "Definitely needs some work," he said.

"Okay Robert, try the clutch pedal now," prompted Jonathan.

Robert worked the pedal up and down.

"Okay, that's enough," replied Jonathan.

Robert shifted the stiff old gearshift lever back and forth. Next, he switched on the headlights. *ZAP!* He heard a clang from the rear of the vehicle as Grandpa flinched and dropped his screwdriver.

"Sorry Grandpa," apologized Robert, "I didn't know you were working on that circuit."

"It's all right, son," said Grandpa, catching his breath and looking for his screwdriver. "I thought I was finally done with this old bucket of bolts."

Robert pulled both steering levers back and latched them in place. After cleaning a chicken nest off the top of the transmission to his right, he bumped his head on the hatch above him. "Aye-yiy-yiy," Robert said, rubbing his head.

"Don't break Grandpa's tractor," kidded Jonathan.

"That's not what I'm worried about," replied Robert, smiling painfully.

Jonathan discovered a jug of black liquid in the engine compartment. "Where do you want us to put this used engine oil, Grandpa?" he asked.

"You can just dump it on the dirt driveway," directed Grandpa. "It'll help keep the dust down."

"Grandpa, we can't do that," said Robert. "It'll pollute the soil!"

Grandpa started to say something but held his tongue. "You're right, Robert," he admitted. "There are still some things an old coot like me can learn. I suppose we can save the oil to lubricate some of the machinery around here."

Robert grinned at his grandpa. "Now you're talking."

It was early evening by the time they were ready to test-drive the tractor. Grandpa gave Jonathan the honors of being the first one to drive it. Jonathan climbed into the driver's seat. Grandpa sat in the assistant driver's position and Robert was behind them both.

When Jonathan pushed the starter button, the old engine cranked over hard and begrudgingly sputtered to life. He waited a few minutes for the engine to warm up, clicked on the headlights, put the tractor in gear, and eased it out of the storage shed. With a loud "tracked vehicle" rumble, he drove through the orchard, testing the different gears as he went.

"Your turn, Robert," said Jonathan as he brought the heavy machine to a halt near the driveway.

"All right!" said Robert as he climbed into the driver's seat. "I've always wanted to drive this thing."

Robert drove around the ranch house a couple of times and then parked out in front. Grandma, Tim, Kimberly, and Lindy came out to see what all the ruckus was. They saw Jonathan,

Robert, and Grandpa climbing out of the big, box-shaped tractor which had large tracks instead of wheels.

"Grandpa?" called out Lindy. "Where did you get this old tractor?"

"I bought it at an army surplus auction many years ago," replied Grandpa. "It's an old U.S. Army 'Stuart' tank. It used to have a turret on it, but I took it off to try to improve its gas mileage."

"Cool, it still works!" exclaimed Tim, eyeing the dusty vehicle with increased attention. "Do you still have the turret?"

"It's probably still around," Grandpa replied. "I think we might have used it as a chicken coop."

"Oh," said Tim, slightly less interested.

Grandpa put his hand on Jonathan's shoulder and said, "Did I ever tell you kids about the time I drove a tank like this during the war?"

"You mean the time you knocked over the water tower?" laughed Jonathan.

"Well, that's part of it. You see, it was like this," began Grandpa.

"You can tell us all about it over dinner, Honey," smiled Grandma as she took him by the arm and they all walked into the house.

CHAPTER 6

Angry Crop Duster

The next morning, Jonathan saw Grandpa out in front of the ranch house talking with a visitor.

"Hi Jonathan, this is Mr. Stilt," introduced Grandpa as Jonathan walked out to meet them. "Mr. Stilt, this is my grandson, Jonathan."

"Glad to meet you, Jonathan," said Mr. Stilt as he shook Jonathan's hand.

"Mr. Stilt has a new crop dusting business in the area," said Grandpa.

"Yes, I was just telling your grandpa that I'd like his business. I'm willing to spray his crops the first time for free."

"I appreciate the offer," said Grandpa, "but we just don't need your services at this time."

"Well, can I sign you up for the middle of the month, then?" pressed Mr. Stilt.

"No thanks, I'm happy with the people we already have," answered Grandpa.

Mr. Stilt's smile suddenly disappeared. "I don't think you understand. The local crop duster's out of commission—I mean—business," he said, his voice growing louder. "I'm offering to do it for free!"

"I work more by personal referral," Grandpa replied. "Get Jeb Carter's backing and talk with me again sometime. Good day."

The salesman scowled and walked back to his truck. Grandpa led Jonathan back toward the house as Mr. Stilt started his pickup.

"Some people don't know a good thing when they hear it!" Mr. Stilt shouted angrily and drove away.

Jonathan and Grandpa watched the salesman's truck roar down the road toward the highway.

"Grandpa, why didn't you take him up on the free crop dusting?" asked Jonathan.

"It just sounded too good to be true," Grandpa responded. "And when something sounds *too good* to be true, Jonathan, you'd better be careful. In life, there is no such thing as *a free lunch.* Somebody's got to pay for it."

Later that afternoon, Grandpa and the cousins were working together repairing the irrigation lines in the orchard. The peaceful mountain air was suddenly interrupted by the peal of a ringing bell.

The cousins looked at each other in surprise and then at their Grandpa. "Too early for the dinner bell," said Grandpa. "Must be something else."

Grandpa picked up his tools and he and the cousins hurried up to the house. The family had a rule that the ranch bell was only to be rung at mealtimes unless there was some kind of emergency.

As Grandpa and the cousins came within sight of the house, Grandma called out to them from the front yard, "It's Mr. Martinez, he's missing!"

"What?" exclaimed Grandpa, breaking into a run.

"Sylvia Martinez called," Grandma explained. "Juan didn't come in for breakfast or lunch. She went out looking for him but couldn't find him anywhere. I told her you'd be over to help look for him."

"Of course I will," said Grandpa. "Juan's a good friend."

"Can we go too?" asked Lindy.

"Sure, but I have to leave right now," said Grandpa.

Within sixty seconds, Grandpa and the cousins had piled into Grandpa's pickup and backed out of the driveway.

"You be careful!" Grandma called out after them.

"Hold down the fort, Honey," returned Grandpa. "We'll be back before dinner."

Fifteen minutes later, Grandpa and the cousins arrived at the Martinez's house. As they pulled into the driveway, Juan's wife, Sylvia, came out to meet them. "Thank you for coming," she said. "I'm worried about Juan. I've looked everywhere for him!"

"Did he have anything he needed to do in town?" asked Grandpa.

"No, he told me he would be working around the ranch all day," said Sylvia.

"How about business appointments?"

"No, I checked his schedule book," said Sylvia. "It was blank for today. The only thing I could find was a note on his desk. I'll show it to you."

Mrs. Martinez led Grandpa and the cousins into Juan's home office. She picked up a piece of scratch paper stapled to an old newspaper article. "Juan wrote today's date and 8 A.M. on this front paper," she said, "and the second page has an article about an old train. It's all I've been able to find."

Grandpa looked at the article for a minute. "Kids, did the train you chased the other day look anything like this?"

The cousins looked at the picture with astonishment. Grandpa was holding up a picture of *the ghost train!*

CHAPTER 7

The Great Train Hold-Up

"That's the ghost train we saw!" exclaimed Tim.

"Sylvia," asked Grandpa, "did Juan ever talk to you about the train in this picture?"

"No," Sylvia replied.

Just then, one of Juan's ranch hands burst into the house. "Mrs. Martinez," he said, "I spotted the tractor out in the east pasture. Thought you'd want to know before I go out there to check on it."

"I'll go with you," said Grandpa as he prepared to leave. "You kids stay here and help Sylvia. I'll be right back."

Grandpa rode with the ranch hand to the deserted tractor. When they arrived, they found that Juan was nowhere in sight. The ranch hand climbed up onto the tractor. "Everything looks okay," he announced from the driver's seat, "the key's even in the ignition." He turned on the key and the tractor started up with a roar.

"No problem with the tractor," Grandpa called out. "Maybe Juan's out checking on the fence."

While Grandpa and the ranch hand searched the region around the tractor, the cousins called a quick huddle inside the Martinez house to discuss the ghost train picture.

"I think we'd better check it out," said Kimberly. "Remember how Grandpa got so worried about the train?"

38

"Yeah," said Tim, "maybe the ghost train people have kidnapped Mr. Martinez and have him tied up on the train."

"They're definitely hiding something," said Robert. "Otherwise, more people would have known about it, and that's Bureau of Land Management land. I say we stop that train and check it out!"

"Okay," Jonathan agreed. "But this time, let's go prepared. We're going to need a chainsaw."

"There's still a chainsaw and fuel in the back of Grandpa's truck," said Robert. "I was using it yesterday to clear out some of the dead trees."

"Great," said Jonathan. "Let's go. Lindy, you stay with Mrs. Martinez. Tell Grandpa we'll be back in a little while."

"What if he asks where you are?" called out Lindy.

"Tell him," said Robert, "that we're goin' to catch a ghost train."

"All aboard!" said Jonathan as he revved up the old pickup and headed out of the driveway.

The cousins drove northeast toward Coldwater Stream and the old logging railroad tracks. Their plan was to drop a small tree across the tracks to stop the train long enough for them to see if Mr. Martinez was on board. The road took them above the valley floor. They could see far up the canyon and spied the train moving among the trees, heading slowly down the canyon.

After several minutes of driving, Jonathan pulled the pickup into a grove of pine trees near the rails at a point halfway between the *Glory-Be* mine and the 50-stamp mill. As the cousins piled out, Robert grabbed the chainsaw and raced over to the railroad tracks. Tim followed. Reaching the tracks, Tim leaned down and put his ear to one of the rails.

"Tim, what are you doing?" asked Kimberly.

"I'm listening for the ghost train. I saw some cowboys do this once in a movie."

"Does it work?" asked Kimberly.

"I don't know," Tim replied. "Every time I put my head down, a frog jumps on my nose."

After selecting a good blockading tree, one that was already dead, Robert set the choke on the chainsaw and pulled the starter rope.

"Go away, frog," exclaimed Tim, "my nose is not a frog house!"

"Hurry up, Robert," urged Kimberly. "The train could be here any minute!"

"I'm trying," returned Robert, pulling the cord handle again and again. The chainsaw finally sputtered to life. Robert pushed the choke off and revved the engine. Wasting no time, he began cutting a notch on the ten-inch diameter tree to direct its fall toward the tracks. When the notch was out, he cut on the backside of the trunk. "Timber!" he yelled.

Everyone scrambled out of the way as the tree leaned over and fell in the wrong direction. "Oops," said Robert, shaking his head.

"Everybody grab a branch," called out Jonathan. "We've got to get this tree across the tracks. That train will be here any minute."

The four cousins pushed and pulled to roll the big tree back toward the railway tracks.

"I think I hear the ghost train coming!" said Tim, trying to help. "Get away, frog! Get away!"

"Everybody push at the same time," directed Jonathan. "One, two, three!"

The cousins gave a final, combined push and the tall pine tree rolled over onto the tracks.

"Goose, I mean, duck!" warned Tim. "Here comes the train."

The cousins dove into the underbrush to wait. "Sure hope

this works," whispered Kimberly.

"Me too," said Jonathan, handing Kimberly the truck keys. "You go and get the truck ready for us to leave in a hurry if we need to. If we're not there in ten minutes, drive the truck back to the Martinez place to meet Grandpa. We'll meet you there."

The chugging of the train suddenly grew louder as the train rounded the bend and came into view. The old black locomotive was pulling four hopper cars loaded with rock.

"There's a tree on the tracks!" yelled a voice from within the train. Locomotive wheels squealed as the engineer braked hard and the train came to a stop thirty feet away from the downed tree.

"Thought you said you had the tracks clear," the cousins heard a man's voice complain.

"Just get that tree out of the way!" barked a second gruff voice from within the locomotive cab. "Nabbing that nosey Martinez guy really messed up our schedule."

"It *was* them," whispered Kimberly to the others.

A short, stocky man jumped down from the locomotive and tried to move the blocking tree. He pushed and pulled but couldn't budge it.

"Do I have to do everything?" grumbled a second, quite-a-bit taller man as he climbed down from the cab.

Jonathan and the other cousins waited anxiously until the second man reached the tree and began trying to move it.

"Now!" motioned Jonathan.

Kimberly raced back for the pickup and Tim, Robert, and Jonathan dashed over to the running locomotive and climbed aboard its platform. They tried the cab door, but it wouldn't open.

"Robert, you and Tim get this door open and see if Mr. Martinez is in the cab," said Jonathan. "There's something tarped in the third car back. I'll go check there."

Jonathan leapt down from the locomotive and ran to the third car. Finding the car's ladder, he climbed up and found the back half of the car covered with the securely tied tarp. As he started to untie the ropes, the train suddenly lunged forward, throwing him onto his stomach.

"Hey, what's going on?!" said Jonathan, getting back up to his hands and knees. He glanced forward and saw Robert and Tim hanging onto the locomotive handrail for dear life. The train was moving.

Hearing the couplers between the cars clank, the short man looked back toward the train. "Lookout!" he yelled. "The brake's failed again!"

"I thought I told you to fix that," said the tall man as both men scrambled to get out of the way.

"I'm *not* maintenance," replied the short man.

The heavy train accelerated forward, pushed the dead tree aside as if it was nothing, and continued picking up speed as it went down the track.

"Stop that train!" shouted the tall man as he and the short man fought to untangle themselves from the brushed-aside tree. Finally breaking loose, the two men got to the tracks and chased after their runaway train now 200 feet ahead of them.

Jonathan, on the third car from the locomotive, finally got enough of the tarp free to see what he needed: Mr. Martinez wasn't there. He looked back at the fourth car; he wasn't there, either.

The train was moving faster now. The cars were beginning to sway side-to-side. Jonathan glanced ahead to the locomotive, realizing he was going to have to jump from car-to-car to get there. He made his way to the front end of the third car. Crouching, he looked down at the speeding ground below, looked at the top edge of the second car four feet away and jumped for it. He landed on the rock and dirt piled in it and sprawled out, trying to keep from falling off. Getting his balance, he crawled to the front of the car.

The train was going faster. Jonathan got ready and jumped again. The front car pitched just as he landed on it, throwing him off-balance. He desperately flailed about for something to grab onto as he tumbled over the side of the car.

Robert and Tim, still trying to get the cab door open, turned just in time to see him fall. "*No!*" shouted Robert.

Jonathan's hands caught hold of the top rail and his body slammed into the steel side. He clung there for a moment, catching his breath, and then started pulling himself back up. Robert and Tim were relieved when they saw his head peek up over the side.

Jonathan climbed back up onto the top of the car and shakily made his way to the front of it.

Robert stepped to the middle of the platform, where part of the handrail was missing, grabbed the steel railing post beside him, and extended his hand out to Jonathan.

Getting to his feet, Jonathan reached forward, grabbed Robert's wrist, and jumped as Robert pulled him onto the rear platform of the locomotive.

"Good catch," Robert called out above the roar of the train.

"Thanks," said Jonathan, his heart still pounding from jumping between the cars. "Juan wasn't under the tarp. It was a bunch of county parking meters."

Tim was standing at the rear door to the locomotive. "We didn't do this," he said. "This locomotive started moving all by itself."

"I know," said Jonathan. "Let's just get this thing stopped so we can get off without breaking our necks."

"I just saw the kidnappers climbing onto the last car," said Robert. "We've got to hurry."

The three boys pushed and pulled and finally got the

locomotive door open. Jonathan and Tim searched for Juan Martinez while Robert studied the controls.

"We just have to cut the throttle and apply the brakes," said Robert.

"Yeah, but which lever is the throttle, and which one is the brakes?" asked Tim, looking up from under a bench seat.

"It's just like the amusement park train back home except ten times bigger," Robert replied. "You just pull down on the throttle here, and—."

Robert had a surprised look on his face when the throttle lever rocked forward and fell off into his hand. "The throttle's still stuck wide open!" he said in alarm.

"Try the brake," yelled Jonathan.

Robert looked around. "It must be this one," he said, pulling back on a lever. The brake lever fell off into his hands, too.

"This locomotive's a mess!" said Robert, frantically trying to put the brake lever back on. "Full throttle, no brakes, and two kidnappers on the train, what *more* can happen?"

"The two kidnappers just jumped to the third car. They're getting closer!" Tim warned from the rear door window.

The train swayed side-to-side as it continued down the old tracks and trees were sweeping by faster and faster as they picked up speed.

"Juan's not on this train and we're getting really close to the 50-stamp mill!" warned Jonathan. "We're going to have to jump."

"Not again," said Tim. "I'm still dizzy from the last time."

As the train entered the last curve before the washed-out Mill Bridge, the two kidnappers jumped from the third to the second hopper car. There was now only one car between the cousins and Juan's kidnappers.

The cousins spied a big field of tall grass. "This looks awfully familiar for some reason," yelled Robert, as he, Tim, and Jonathan jumped from the speeding train. They tucked their heads to protect themselves and rolled head-over-heels through the dense meadow-grass.

"It's a bunch of brat kids!" shouted the tall man from the train.

Tim caught a glimpse of the angry man's face just before everything went dark.

CHAPTER 8

Missing Tracks

Tim's world was spinning. He dreamed he was on a giant rollercoaster, not wearing a seatbelt. The rollercoaster suddenly jumped the track and Tim's car went flying through the air. Down, down it fell. It landed in a field of tall weeds. Tim felt something tap him on the back of his neck. He turned his head and shouted, "Termites! They're eating the railroad ties! We're all going to–." ***Wham!***

A blindingly bright light appeared. Tim closed his eyes. His head hurt. When Tim opened his eyes again, he was confused. "What...what happened?" he said. "Where am I?" He sat up and ouchfully felt a large bump on the back of his head.

"Easy, little brother," said Kimberly, sitting at his side. "Everything's going to be okay."

Tim glanced around at his new surroundings. He was back in his bed at Grandma and Grandpa's house.

"Hey everyone, Tim's awake!" Kimberly called out. Soon, Tim's concerned grandparents and cousins were at his side.

Tim spied the window. "It's dark outside?" he asked.

"Take it easy, Tim," said Jonathan. "You hit your head on a small tree when we jumped from the train."

"Yeah, you should have seen that poor tree," added Robert. "You broke it right in two."

"Better the tree than his head," said Grandma, relieved to

have Tim awake. "The doctor said you'd be okay, just really sore."

"What about the ghost train?" asked Tim.

"It's disappeared again," said Jonathan. "We had to hide from the two kidnapper men. Kimberly met us with the pickup, so we didn't see what happened to it."

"We lost the train again?" said Tim, laying his head back down on his pillow. "That's really...unusual."

"We had to choose our battle, Tim," Jonathan said. "Making sure you were okay was more important than continuing to pursue the train with the pickup."

"That train was a mechanical mess anyways," said Robert. "I bet nobody's done any maintenance on it for years. It should be banned from the tracks until its fixed."

"Tim," said Kimberly, apologetically, "I am really glad you're okay. I mean, I shouldn't have come up with the idea to stop the train. And, well, I'm sorry I called you a pest."

"That's okay," said Tim, looking at his sister with a weak grin. "I mean, that's what big sisters are for, right? To be annoying...sometimes?"

Kimberly grinned back. "I want to help you...I'm going to help you survive into your twenties. I promise."

The next morning at breakfast, Tim was up and around, and, as Grandpa put it, "he was hungry as a bear just out of hibernation." Grandpa informed the cousins that the sheriff's deputies had joined in the search for Juan Martinez and were also looking for the ghost train men.

After breakfast, the cousins helped with the dishes. Robert and Lindy teamed up on the washing, Tim rinsed, and Jonathan and Kimberly dried. Tim was halfway done rinsing a frying pan when the sink faucet made a gurgling sound. "Hey, who took all the water?" he complained.

"Grandma," Kimberly called out to her grandmother in the

dining room, "the water's gone off."

"It's probably the pipes," said Grandma. "Remember, they get clogged with iron if we don't clean them out regularly. Just like last summer."

"Sounds like a wonderful job for the boys," volunteered Lindy. Grandma agreed.

"Gee, thanks Lindy," said Robert.

"Anytime, dear twin brother," Lindy smilingly teased him.

"Tell you what," said Grandma. "You boys fix the water and the girls and I will pull the weeds in the garden." This time it was Robert that got to do the smiling. "The first group that gets done," continued Grandma, "will get some homemade ice cream."

"It's a deal," said Robert, accepting the challenge. "Too bad you girls are going to miss out on Grandma's homemade ice cream."

After gathering pipe wrenches and other tools, Robert, Jonathan, and Tim set out to locate the water problem.

The water for the ranch house came from a natural spring on the mountainside above the house. From the spring, it flowed through an old inch-and-a-half diameter iron pipe into a large, concrete storage cistern. From there, it gravity-flowed through another pipe down to the house.

When the boys got to the cistern, they opened the access door and found the huge, basement-like water tank nearly empty. "It's clogged somewhere between here and the spring," said Jonathan.

As the three boys continued following the pipeline up the hill, they came across several faucets and tried each of them for water.

"No water at this one either," Tim announced.

"The next place to check is the spring tunnel," said Jonathan. "I sure hope the spring hasn't gone dry."

The cousins hiked up a narrow ravine and came to a small stream of water flowing on the ground. Following the stream, they soon came to its source at the spring tunnel, where a small waterfall was flowing out from under the old, green wooden door. Unlatching the door, the boys peered into the humid spring tunnel. The tunnel was about fifteen feet long, seven feet tall, and hewn out of solid rock. It had an arch-shaped ceiling. The water in the tunnel was about a foot deep. The spring water was coming from a narrow crack in the left-hand wall and flowed into the pool.

"Plenty of water in there," said Jonathan, sizing up the situation, "the pipe must be plugged somewhere between here and that first faucet just down the hill. Let's get to work."

Using their pipe wrenches, the boys removed a plug from a clean-out tee in the pipe and started rodding out the pipe with a clean plumbers' snake. Tim was sent back down the hill to the nearest faucet to make sure it was turned on.

"Nothing yet," Tim called out to the others.

Robert and Jonathan continued working the long metal snake back and forth to unplug the pipe.

Tim crouched down impatiently to look into the opening of the water faucet. "Come on, water, let's get going," he said, anxious to win the homemade ice cream race.

Without warning, rusty-orange water suddenly gushed from the faucet, spraying Tim's face and shirt. "Whew, that water's cold!" he gasped, backing out of the way. "Hey guys, the line's not blocked anymore!" Tim left the water running until it turned clear and then shut it off.

At the spring tunnel entrance, Robert and Jonathan were hurrying to re-assemble the water pipes.

"Jonathan," Robert said as he spied an orange Tim heading up the hill, "don't look now, but I think the dreaded *Rust Monster* is coming after us."

"Funny, very funny," Tim replied, still wringing water from his shirt. "Hurry up you guys, we've got to beat the girls."

The three boys grabbed up their tools and raced back down the hill. When they got to the house, they found Grandma and the girls still in the garden, but just finishing their weeding.

"We won!" announced Tim with a big grin. "Oh, boy, that homemade ice cream is sure going to taste good."

"You still have to put your tools away," said Kimberly.

"But that wasn't part of the deal," protested Tim.

Jonathan grabbed Tim by the arm. "Come on," he said, "we can still beat them."

The three boys ran to the garage, dropped off their tools, and dashed for the dining room, beating the girls by three seconds.

"Yahoo, we won!" called out Tim and Robert, breaking into a victory dance. Kimberly and Lindy were protesting.

"I declare a tie!" said Grandma, holding up her hands, trying to avert an all-out war.

"Aw, Grandma," said Jonathan, "you just want some ice cream, too."

"Of course," said Grandma with a smile, "homemade ice cream is my favorite. Now into the kitchen, all of you."

With bowls heaping, the cousins and their grandparents filed into the dining room to enjoy their cool treat.

Kimberly eyed Robert's bowl of ice cream. "Robert, what kind of topping did you get?"

"It's great," replied Robert, holding up a spoonful. "You've *got* to try it."

"It looks like chili beans," said Kimberly.

Robert took a big bite. "Good guess. Chili beans are great with vanilla ice cream. A friend at camp told me about it."

Robert tried to convince them all how *wonderful* the ice cream tasted, but for some strange reason, none of the others wanted to even *taste* the brown goo.

While they were eating their ice cream, Lindy had been carefully glancing through great-great Grandpa Jake's farm book containing the clue.

"Wait a minute, Robert," Lindy said, moving the book over so Robert could see it, too. "There's something wrong with this date. See, here, it says, 'Water problems 7/11/15—Page 49."

"What's wrong with that?" asked Robert.

"Look at the title page," said Lindy. "*Farm Resource Company, Copyright, 1919.* This book wasn't even printed until 1919."

"But why would Grandpa Jake write a date in the front of the book referring to something four years *before* the book was even published?" asked Robert.

"I'm not sure," said Lindy thoughtfully as she thumbed through the book to find page forty-nine. But this time, page forty-nine was missing!

"Wait a minute," said Robert. "It was there before. I looked at it during breakfast."

"Oh, here it is," said Lindy, carefully prying the pages apart. "Looks like someone spilled something on it and the pages got stuck together."

"Oops!" said Robert.

"Listen to this," said Lindy, reading from page 49. "Apple vinegar can be used to clean rust off of iron implements and machinery springs—. Page 49 and a strange date written in the front of the book. That's all the clue we've got."

"Maybe he wrote the wrong year," said Robert.

"Or maybe it's not a date at all," said Lindy, her eyes lightening. "Maybe it's word-numbers!"

"Word-numbers?" said Robert.

By this time, Grandma, Grandpa, and all the other cousins were gathered around and listening in.

"Page 49, word numbers 7, 11, and 15," said Lindy. "Let's

see—'Apple vinegar'—one, two—'can be used'—three, four, five—to *clean*—six, seven—rust off of **iron**—eleven—implements and machinery *springs*.' That's it!" Lindy said excitedly. "***Clean iron springs!***"

"We have to soak the iron springs in vinegar?" asked Tim. "They'll stink for a week."

"Not springs," said Kimberly. "*The* iron springs. You know, the wonderful orange stuff you've got all over your face and shirt."

"Oh," said Tim, "you mean that the spring tunnel might be the mine?"

"Well what are we waiting for?" said Grandpa with a big grin on his face. "Let's go find out!"

Grandma, Grandpa, and the cousins quickly rounded up safety hard hats, flashlights, water buckets, shovels, brooms, picks, and other tools, and hurried up to the old spring tunnel. Since the water from the spring was used to fill the ranch cistern, Grandpa and Jonathan removed a pipe plug in the water line to let the spring water flow out into the ravine rather than into the cistern. That way they could keep the water in the cistern pure and unmuddied while they worked in the spring tunnel. They also switched on their supplemental well pump to keep filling the cistern with clean water as they worked.

Jonathan and Robert went into the spring tunnel first. They slipped on rubber boots and, using shovels and buckets, started to work cleaning the water, sand, gravel, and rust-colored iron sediment from the floor of the old tunnel. Grandpa, Grandma, and the other cousins waited eagerly outside the tunnel.

"Stay clear of the opening," Grandpa urged the others. "They're going to be bucketing a lot of stuff out this way."

Six inches down, Jonathan and Robert discovered two parallel pipes caked with rust.

"Be careful," said Grandpa, "it might be the top to a shaft or something."

"Hold on," said Jonathan, "these aren't pipes."

"What did he say?" asked Grandma from outside the tunnel.

"They found two rusty things that aren't pipes," Lindy informed her.

"Oh," said Grandma. "That's nice."

"They look more like railroad tracks," added Jonathan.

Jonathan and Robert kept digging and bucketing out the sludge to expose the rails. "The tracks seem to be heading toward the back wall of the tunnel," said Jonathan.

"Not just toward it," said Robert. "Look, they go *into* it. Grandpa, come here and take a look!"

Already wearing his rubber boots, Grandpa switched on his hard hat light and stepped into the tunnel. "Let's see," he said, walking back to where Robert was shining his flashlight. The rails did indeed appear to go right into the rock at the end of the tunnel. There was rock there, but also concrete.

"Somebody get me a pick," Grandpa said excitedly. A pick was passed in from outside the tunnel. "Stand back boys," directed Grandpa. "Let's see where these tracks go."

Robert hadn't seen his grandfather this excited in years.

Grandpa leaned back and took a swing with the pick. *Clang!* He leaned back and swung harder. *Clang!* He swung again. This time sparks and rock-chips flew. He swung again and again. Soon sweating heavily in the humid tunnel, Grandpa paused. "Robert," he said, "have them send in the sledgehammer."

The cousins passed in the sledgehammer and Grandpa set back to work.

Wham! Wham! Wham! The rock shuddered.

Wham! Wham! Wham! Cracks appeared in the thick stone and concrete wall.

Wham! Grandpa swung with all his might. *Wham!*

The top third of the wall crumbled and fell backwards,

revealing a dark chasm!

CHAPTER 9

The Lost Gold Mine?

"Robert, let me borrow your flashlight," said Grandpa Charlie excitedly.

"What do you see?" asked Grandma anxiously from outside.

"A tunnel. It keeps on going as far as I can see!"

"Yahoo!" shouted the cousins.

"Can I see?" said Tim.

"Let me knock a little more off the wall," said Grandpa. He resumed sledgehammering the wall in earnest. In a matter of minutes, he had made a four-foot-tall opening they could easily climb through.

Grandpa set his sledgehammer down and wiped the perspiration from his brow. "This is incredible," he said, "after all these years, the lost mine was right in my own backyard. In our own spring tunnel!"

The water was shallower in the spring tunnel now. The cousins' bucketing had worked well. Jonathan and Robert laid several wooden planks down along the floor to form a footbridge over the remaining water.

After allowing the air in the tunnel to clear, Grandpa and the five cousins, flashlights in hand, climbed over the wall and into the dark tunnel beyond. Grandma stayed at the entry.

In sharp contrast to the spring tunnel, the floor of the old mine was bone dry. It took a moment for their eyes to get used to the darkness and then they began following the mine car tracks down the tunnel. The tunnel was about four-and-a-half feet wide and seven feet tall. It appeared to be all hand-dug with a pick because pick mark gouges were still visible in the ceiling and walls.

After fifty feet, Grandpa and the cousins came to side tunnels on the left and right. Grandpa shined his flashlight down the one on the left. "There isn't any track in this side tunnel," he said, "so I don't suspect it goes too far. We'll check it out, though."

The left tunnel ended abruptly after twenty-five feet. There was a narrow, white quartz vein showing at the end. Lindy, interested in geology, studied the quartz vein closely.

"Not a whole lot of gold so far, is there," said Robert, looking at the vein with her.

"No, but this quartz is the right kind of rock," Lindy replied. "That's where they would find the gold."

Grandpa and the cousins next explored the tunnel on the right. It also ended abruptly after twenty feet.

After returning to the main tunnel, they continued to follow the tracks. The tunnel curved slightly to the left. Kimberly glanced back over her shoulder and could see no trace of light from the entrance. "If anybody suggests that we turn off our flashlights to see how dark it is," she said, looking directly at Tim, "I think I will personally bean them."

"But Kimberly," said Tim, "that's what you're *supposed* to do in dark tunnels. It makes you glad for the light."

The tunnel continued for about 240 feet and then ended in a "T". At the junction, there was a turntable to enable a mine car to be switched onto the tracks going to the right or to the left. Grandpa and the cousins followed the tunnel to the right. After walking for seventy feet, they came to an area where the walls and ceiling were "shored-up" with wood. There were "sets"—two 12"x12" wooden posts with a "cap" beam across the top of them at the ceiling—holding the 4"x12" planks in place in the ceilings and walls. There was a small wooden door halfway up on the wall to the right.

"What's that?" asked Tim.

"Probably an ore chute," answered Grandpa. "Stand back while I open it."

Grandpa cautiously unlatched the door. It hinged downward. With a rumble, some dirt and rocks tumbled out of the chute and landed on the tunnel floor.

After the dust had cleared, they looked up into the ore chute. "Wow, this would make a great slide," said Robert.

"They used ore chutes to drop rock from a higher tunnel down into an empty mine car below," Grandpa explained. "Saved them from having to double-handle the ore."

"You know," quipped Tim, "if they had two ore chutes here, we'd have a pair-a-chutes."

"Parachutes?" returned Jonathan with a grin. "Back to the drawing boards, Tim."

The tunnel was shored with wood timbers for the next thirty feet. At the end of the shoring, Grandpa and the cousins emerged into a large room. The ceiling angled upwards and back over the tunnel from which they had just emerged. The room was roughly fifteen feet wide by seventy feet long.

Jonathan directed his light at the ceiling twenty-five feet above them. "A *little* gold mine?" he said. "Somebody's sure done a lot of work here."

"This is a lot bigger diggings than I ever dreamed," said Grandpa in amazement.

Tim and Robert climbed up into the large, sloping room above. "Here's the top of the ore chute," Tim called down.

"Why don't you guys just 'parachute' down," kidded Kimberly.

"Ha!" replied Tim.

"What was that?" chuckled Robert.

"Half a *ha-ha*," said Tim.

After Robert and Tim had explored the upper level, they climbed back down to where the others were waiting.

"It dead-ends up there a-ways," informed Robert. "There weren't any more tunnels that we could see. Let's go check out the other branch of the 'T'."

Grandpa and the cousins retraced their steps back to the "T" and this time took the left branch. The tunnel went straight for sixty feet and then began to curve to the right. It was a "drift" tunnel, meaning that the miners had dug it "drifting after" or following the gold vein. Once again, they came to an area that was heavily shored with large, wooden timbers. This time, not just the walls and ceiling were shored, but the floor was made of heavy planks as well. Ten feet further, on the left, was another ore chute, and just beyond that, was a ladder going up through a trap door in the tunnel ceiling.

Grandpa cautiously climbed up the ladder and discovered another large room above the tunnel. The room, or "stope", sloped upwards where the miners had dug out the gold vein. He found a simple hoist that the miners had rigged to help them lift their tools into the room above. Grandpa didn't touch the ropes, just in case they were fragile. There were mine car tracks on this upper level as well. He walked the length of the tracks in both directions. There were timbers in many locations, both to support the tracks and also to keep the large room from sloughing in.

As Grandpa was returning to the ladder, he spied an old miner's drift pick leaning against the right-hand wall of the tunnel. Next to it was an old round-nosed, rivetted shovel. Both tools were covered with the dust of perhaps a hundred years. Beside them was a large rock, its top surface about chair height.

Curious, Grandpa Charlie walked over to examine the tools more closely. He adjusted his helmet's headlamp and lifted the drift pick. The pick had a well-balanced feel to it, not too heavy, not too light. It felt good in his hands.

Grandpa wiped the dust off the old pick. There was something carved into the old hickory-wood handle: a "K", or an "R". He wiped more dust off. A jolt went through his system when he recognized the word "JAKE" carved into the handle. Tears suddenly came to his eyes. He sat down on the rock, just staring at the name. "Grandpa Jake," he said aloud, his mind filling with memories of family fun. "Good ol' Grandpa Jake."

Down in the main tunnel, the Wright cousins were getting anxious to move on.

"I'm going to check on Grandpa," said Jonathan, starting up the ladder. When he reached the top, he spied Grandpa sitting down, still looking at the well-worn pick. "Grandpa, are you okay?"

"Yes, son," Grandpa Charlie replied, clearing his throat. "This is my Grandpa's mine, all right. I just found his pick and shovel. He dug this place. Boy, what hard work he went through to get our family started. I had no idea."

Grandpa Charlie had the rest of the cousins come up to see the tools and visit the large room. As they were heading back down by way of the ladder, Tim said, "Shouldn't we bring the pick and shovel with us?"

"Not yet," said Grandpa, "I want to make sure the handles won't fall apart when we get them out of the mine. They've been in this specific atmosphere for so long, we may have to stabilize or protect the wood by coating it with something. I don't want to lose Grandpa Jake's carving."

When they were all back down and ready, Grandpa and the cousins continued along the main tunnel. The tunnel turned sharply to the right and they soon found their way blocked by a locked, thick wooden door. Shining their lights, they looked it over.

"These hinges were hand-wrought by a blacksmith," said Grandpa. "The same with the hasp and loop."

"Do you think Grandpa Jake made them?" asked Robert.

"He could have," Grandpa Charlie replied. "He had his own blacksmithing forge."

A large brass and iron lock secured the door shut. Grandpa and the cousins tried picking the lock but couldn't; no one even had a bobby pin. They tried forcing the door open with their shoulders, but the door refused to budge.

"Whatever's behind there will just have to wait until we can get some better tools," Grandpa said reluctantly.

"I think I'm inclined to agree with you," added Jonathan, rubbing the soreness from his shoulder.

The group followed the tracks back to the "T", turned right, and soon arrived back at the spring tunnel wall. As they climbed over the wall, they spied Grandma still sitting near the entrance to the spring tunnel and quickly went out to talk with her.

"What did you find?" asked Grandma.

"Grandpa found a drift pick with the name 'Jake' carved into its handle," Jonathan said excitedly.

"No gold yet," said Robert, "but we did find a locked door. There's got to be something behind it."

"Grandma," asked Tim, "why didn't you come exploring with us?"

"I'm a little claustrophobic," Grandma replied. "I don't like small, dark places. I'm happy out here in the sunshine."

"We'll tell you all about it," said Robert excitedly. "It's so neat. Tim even found a parachute!"

"That's *pair of chutes*," Kimberly explained.

While the rest of the cousins told their Grandma about the

mine, Grandpa and Tim slipped away to get tools for picking the lock.

Nearing the house, Grandpa and Tim spotted a white "County Department of Land Use" car parked in the driveway. A tall man was knocking on the front door; a second man was sitting in the car looking the place over.

"Oh no," remarked Grandpa impatiently. "What do they want now?!"

CHAPTER 10

Charge of the Light Brigade

Tim stopped at the corner of the house, but Grandpa walked around the front to meet the men. "That guy looks awfully familiar," thought Tim. "Where have I seen him before?"

"Howdy," said Grandpa, "can I help you?"

"Yes," spoke up the tall man at the front door. "We're from the county land use department. We've had reports of a mountain lion being seen in this vicinity. Mind if we take a look around?"

"Afraid you must have the wrong property," said Grandpa. "I haven't seen a mountain lion around these parts for twenty years or more."

"We've also been informed that there's thistle growing in your fields," said the tall man, taking off his sunglasses and wiping the lenses with his handkerchief.

"I'm sorry to disappoint you," said Grandpa. "But I keep a clean ranch. Don't allow any thistle weeds to live around here."

The tall man arrogantly put on his glasses and looked at Grandpa. "You don't mean to say you *purposefully* eradicate thistle plants from your property, do you? That's a very serious offense!"

Tim snuck a peek at the tall stranger from around the corner of the house. He suddenly recognized the man's face. It was the tall man from the *ghost train!*

Tim ducked back behind the house, hoping the man hadn't seen him. If Tim were to try to warn his grandpa, the tall man might see him, and things could get rough.

"Oh boy, what am I going to do?" thought Tim. "I've got to warn the others!" He turned and ran as fast as he could back up to the spring tunnel.

"Where's Grandpa and the tools to open the lock?" called out Robert as Tim came puffing up the hill. Tim tried to motion to Robert to be quiet. When Tim reached Grandma and the cousins at the spring tunnel, he blurted out. "The ghost train guys are here!"

"What?" Jonathan replied. "Where?"

"At the front door of the house," exclaimed Tim. "Grandpa's talking to them—he doesn't know who they are!"

Grandma and the cousins held a quick huddle. The cousins would try to warn Grandpa while Grandma tried to reach a phone to call the sheriff's office. As quickly and quietly as possible, the cousins slipped down the hill to the ranch house. In the front yard, they spotted their grandpa talking to the two men by the county car.

"I'm afraid you'll have to come with us," they overheard the tall man say. "We have some questions we want to ask you."

"Talk to my lawyer," said Grandpa Charlie.

"No, you see, we can't do that," continued the tall man. "Juan Martinez sent us to talk to you. Seems he's in serious trouble with the law."

"Juan's never broken a law in his life," defended Grandpa. "Why, he's never even gotten a speeding ticket!"

"He's broken a serious *environmental* law!" spat the tall man angrily. "He's destroyed nature's balance by planting *human food* crops on these beautiful, scenic mountains. He's planted fruit trees in *straight rows*, and so have you!"

"Environmental law, BALONEY! Man was put here to beautify and improve this earth, not be *erased* from it!" returned Grandpa.

The tall man, livid with anger, pulled out a gun and aimed it at Grandpa. "Get into the car!" he hissed menacingly.

"Oh no!" gasped Kimberly. "They're going to take Grandpa!"

"No way," said Jonathan. "Everyone to the tractor. We'll cut them off at the pass!"

The cousins sprinted over to the barn, pulled off the tarp, and piled into the old army tank. Robert slipped through the forward hatchway and plunked into the driver's seat. He hit the ignition. "Come on, come on, please start," he muttered.

Reluctantly, the stubborn old machine sputtered to life. Robert revved the engine to keep it from stalling.

Kimberly was the last to get there and jumped onto the tank's front armor. "They've got Grandpa in their car!" she yelled.

"Get in, Kimberly," said Jonathan. "We're going to stop them."

Robert accidentally popped the clutch. The tank lunged forward, sending Kimberly tumbling head-over-heels through the round opening in the top of the tank where the turret used to be. Kimberly landed smack on top of Tim behind the driver's seat.

"Help, I'm squished!" complained Tim as the tank roared out of the barn.

"Me too," called out Jonathan from underneath them both. "Could you guys please get off of me."

Lindy was in the assistant driver's seat to Robert's right, spying for movement. "Robert, they're backing out of the house driveway," informed Lindy.

"Hold on, we'll cut them off before they get turned around."

Robert steered the tank straight for the car.

"What is *that*?!" exclaimed the tall man in the county car as he spotted the turretless tank speeding toward them. "Look out, it's going to ram us!"

The driver of the car swerved just in time to evade the tank. He threw the car into drive, then reverse, and then floored it. The cousins in the tank roared past them and turned to block the car, but it was too late. The car had already gotten out of the turnaround and was speeding down the gravelly-dirt driveway.

"We'll have to go cross-country to cut them off by the orchard," said Robert.

"Do you think we can make it?" Kimberly called out, hanging on for dear life as the tank picked up speed.

"Cuz'," said Robert with a serious smile on his face, "this machine was *made* for cross-country."

"Yeehaw! Four-wheel drive!" shouted Tim as they left the graded road and plowed through the orchard.

Robert hit the gas pedal a little too hard and it stuck to the floor. "The throttle's stuck wide-open," he shouted above the roar of the tank. "I can't get the pedal back up!"

"Hang-on everybody!" Jonathan warned. "Here we go *again!*"

"Robert, they're heading toward the rock walls in the orchard," Lindy called out.

The car driver caught sight of the tank on his right and swerved. He over-reacted and sent the car skidding sideways on the gravel.

SMASH! The car slammed into the rock wall embankment to the right of the road. Grandpa kicked the gun out of the tall man's hand, threw open the door, and tumbled from the car.

"Get him!" ordered the tall man to the stunned driver. The two men grabbed their guns and sprang from the damaged car.

"Forget the old man, *look what's coming!*" shouted the driver. He leveled his pistol to aim at the oncoming tank.

"Close the hatches," yelled Kimberly to Robert and Lindy, ducking down. "They're going to shoot at us!"

The youths slammed their hatches shut and switched to periscope just as a bullet pounded on the tank's frontal armor. *Thud! Thud! Twang!* Three more bullets ricocheted in rapid succession.

"This is my kind of tractor!" Robert said with a grin.

"You said it!" Tim agreed, hanging on in the middle of the tank.

With reduced vision, Robert couldn't see the irrigation ditch looming ahead. *WHAM!* The tank hit the ditch hard and bounced through it.

Lindy glanced through her periscope. "The wall!"

SMACK! Rocks flew in every direction as the eleven-ton tank smashed through the three-foot-tall rock wall, flew eight feet through the air, landed with a big crunching sound on top of the kidnappers' car, and kept going.

"Run for it!" shouted the tall man. "They've demolished the car!"

The two crooks fled down the road with the roaring tank hot on their heels. Desperate to get away, the men raced into the orchard on their left, tripped, and fell into the old dry, hand-dug well located there.

Peering over the top of the tank, Kimberly saw the crooks disappear. "They're in the old well," she shouted.

"Are you sure?" returned Robert, trying to rein in the old tank.

"Kimberly's right," Jonathan added.

Robert shut off the engine and braked the tank to a screeching halt. As their trail of dust caught up with them, it suddenly became very, very quiet. After a moment, the cousins peered cautiously over the top of the tank again.

"Robert, you get that throttle unstuck," said Jonathan,

glancing around. "I'm going to go check things out."

"I'm going, too," said Tim.

"No Tim," said Kimberly. "You stay here with us where I can keep an eye on you."

"Aw, Kim," said Tim.

"She's right," said Jonathan. "You've already had one hard conk on your head this week."

"Be careful, Jonathan," said Kimberly as Jonathan started to climb out. "They may still be armed."

Once out of the tank, Jonathan snuck carefully over to the dry well and peered over the edge of its concrete rim. Twenty feet below, the two kidnappers were lying unconscious on the soft, sandy floor of the pit.

"Guess that'll hold them for a while," said Jonathan, and he returned to the tank to inform the others.

"Hey, where's Grandpa?" asked Lindy, pushing open her top hatch.

"Last I saw, he dodged into the trees on the other side of the road," Jonathan replied.

"You kids okay?" called out a familiar voice from the rear of the tractor-tank.

"Grandpa!" exclaimed Kimberly.

The other cousins piled out of the tank and they all ran over to their grandpa and smothered him with hugs.

"Are you okay?" asked Lindy, her voice choked with emotion. "They didn't hurt you or anything, did they?"

"I'm fine, thanks to you kids," Grandpa Charlie replied with a grin. "But mind you, too many more of your bear hugs and I might have to change my answer."

Grandpa looked at the five cousins seriously for a moment. "Hope you kids didn't scratch my rusty paint job on this old tank," he said, and broke into a grin. "Just kidding. You know, it's a good thing we kept this old 'bucket of bolts' after all."

Jonathan and Robert worked on freeing up the gas pedal while Grandpa and the others walked over to the dry well.

"Get us out of here," demanded the groggy tall man from the bottom of the well.

"We'll get you out," replied Grandpa Charlie. "Just as soon as the sheriff gets here."

The sound of a pickup coming down the drive caught their attention. It was Grandma. She stopped the truck near the dry well, got out, and hugged Grandpa tightly. "I'm so glad you're okay, Honey!" she said. "When those wicked men took you away, I thought I might never see you again." She looked at the cousins, the tank, and the smashed kidnapper's car. "Thank goodness you're all okay. The sheriff is on his way."

A few minutes later, the cousins and their grandparents heard a siren and spied the sheriff's car coming up the long ranch driveway. They flagged him down near the old well. The deputy parked his patrol car and climbed out. He looked to be in his mid-forties. "Hello, I'm Deputy Morrison," he said, extending his hand to Grandpa Charlie.

"I'm Charlie Wright," greeted Grandpa. "Thanks for coming."

"The two men in the bottom of that well tried to kidnap our grandpa," blurted out Tim. "And they shot at us, too!"

Grandpa and the cousins quickly told the deputy about the attempted kidnapping. After the officer made several notes, he ordered the two men to empty and throw up their weapons. He gathered the guns and stood guard while Grandpa and the Wright cousins hoisted each of the two men from the well. Deputy Morrison handcuffed and searched the two men.

"We'll be back," snarled the tall man.

"That's enough, mister!" Deputy Morrison ordered. The deputy soon had the men secured in the back seat of his patrol car.

"Grandpa?" asked Tim after the deputy was done. "Do you think Deputy Morrison could help us pick the lock in the mine?"

"Did you guys find Crazy Jake's lost gold mine?" asked the deputy with interest.

Tim was about to say something but Kimberly elbowed him a good one in the ribs.

"We just found an old lock," said Jonathan, trying to answer the question without giving away any more information. "We wanted to try to pick it so we didn't wreck it."

"Oh," replied Deputy Morrison. "I'm afraid I'm not too good at picking locks. You might try the locksmith in town."

"Good idea," said Grandpa. "Have you found my neighbor, Juan Martinez, yet?"

"No," replied the deputy. "But we're calling in more help. We'll find him soon."

"These two creeps mentioned Juan's name to me earlier up at the house," informed Grandpa. "They're the ones who kidnapped him."

"Thanks," said Deputy Morrison. He scratched his head and nodded toward the crooks in the back seat of his patrol car. "We'll find out what their deal is. Those two are definitely up to no good."

Deputy Morrison put on his sunglasses and climbed into the patrol car. "Oh, I'll have a tow truck come for the county car in the morning."

"Thanks," said Grandpa. "Better have them bring a trailer to load it on. I don't think their car rolls very well anymore."

"I see what you mean," smiled the deputy as he glanced at the car and back at the old tank. "It looks like a mighty mean tractor ran over it."

Later that evening, Grandpa, Grandma, and the cousins ate a simple—though somewhat belated—dinner.

"Kids," said Grandpa with emotion in his voice, "I want to thank you for helping me today. You saved my life."

"*You're welcome*," replied the grinning cousins in unison. There were grateful smiles all around.

"By the way," said Tim a few moments later, "when do we get to pick the lock?"

CHAPTER 11

A New Expedition

"Come on kids, let's go pick that lock in the gold mine," said Grandpa bright and early the next morning.

"All right!" said Tim, rolling out of bed, bright and chipper for once.

The cousins quickly got ready and grabbed some hardhats and flashlights. On the way out of the house, they drank some orange juice and snagged the egg sandwiches Grandma had prepared for them.

"Thanks for the breakfast, Grandma," said Robert. "Maybe today we'll find you some real gold nuggets."

A beautiful mountain sunrise was just beginning to glow as Grandpa and the cousins hiked up to the old spring tunnel. After opening the spring tunnel door, they climbed over the rock wall into the lost gold mine.

"The locked room is down the tunnel to the left," said Lindy as they stopped to get their bearings at the "T" in the tracks.

They followed the left-hand tunnel past the old ladder, hoist, and ore chute, and soon arrived at the locked door.

"Shine your lights on the lock," directed Grandpa as he retrieved a screwdriver, a knife, and a few tools with different shaped hooks on the end of them from his small backpack.

The cousins eagerly looked on as Grandpa focused his attention on the old lock. The padlock was four inches tall and three inches wide. Grandpa pivoted the lock's one-inch-tall brass weather panel over to the side to reveal the keyhole. He then put some oil into the lock to free it up and began working with his various tools, poking them into the keyhole, pushing, pulling, and twisting. Something inside the lock finally clicked, and the hinged link fell open.

"You did it!" exclaimed Kimberly.

Grandpa removed the lock and slid open the hand-wrought door bolt. Visions of a treasure-filled room filled the cousins' minds as Grandpa tried to pull open the thick wooden door.

CREEEEEK! The old hinges stubbornly resisted as Grandpa, joined by the cousins, struggled to open the door that hadn't been opened in over a hundred years. Grandpa oiled the hinges and they struggled to pull open the door. As they did so, they heard a sliding, thumping sound inside the room.

"What was that?!" asked Lindy.

"Let me out of here!" cried out a muffled voice from within the room.

The cousins jumped back as Grandpa slammed the partially opened door back closed again. There was a scraping sound and then a loud *THUNK!* as someone or something moved inside the room. Then it was quiet, *very* quiet.

"What—*what* was that?" Tim asked, breaking the nervous silence.

"I don't know," said Grandpa in consternation.

"Whatever it is," said Robert. "It's been locked in there for over a hundred years."

"Yeah," said Tim. "And maybe it should be locked in there for a little while longer."

Grandpa picked up a club-like board from the floor of the tunnel. "You kids open the door and then get out of the way. I'll take it from there."

"Help! Let me out of here!" called out the voice again from

72

inside the room. Tim couldn't contain himself any longer and burst into laughter.

"Timothy, I thought it was you!" exclaimed Kimberly. "Your ventriloquism pranks are going to get you into trouble one of these days."

"Boy," laughed Tim, "I really had you guys going for a minute there."

"All in favor of letting Tim open the door," proposed Jonathan, "raise your hands."

Four hands, but not Tim's, shot up in agreement. Tim, assisted by Grandpa, got to tug on the door.

Creek. CLANG!

"Look out!" shouted Tim.

The swinging door conked Grandpa's headlamp and pushed him aside. The cousins lost their flashlights as they jumped out of the way. A large, dark mass swept past them, pursuing a terrorized Tim down the tunnel. The large creature stopped after fifteen feet, but poor Tim kept right on going. He ran clear to the "T" in the tunnel before looking back.

Grandpa and the cousins froze against the walls of the now pitch-dark tunnel to avoid being detected. The darkness was so thick they could feel it.

"Great time to break our flashlights," Robert whispered to Jonathan. "Did you see where they landed?"

"Here's one," whispered Kimberly from across the tunnel. "But the bulb must be burned out. I can't get it to work."

Grrrowwl!

"What was that?!" whispered Jonathan.

"My tummy," chuckled Robert.

"Hey, where is everybody?" called out Tim's timid voice from down the tunnel.

"We're back by the room," answered Grandpa, still brandishing his large wooden club. "Bring your light."

A dim light began to creep into the tunnel as Tim cautiously returned toward them. As the light grew brighter, Grandpa and the cousins caught sight of what had chased them.

"A mine car?" said Robert.

The bright light from a flashlight shined in their eyes as Tim cautiously peeked around the bend of the tunnel. "You guys okay?" he asked.

"Nothing that a little bright light won't cure," Kimberly replied.

"Where'd that come from?" said Tim as he spotted the old, wooden-boxed mine car.

"That's the ferocious beast that almost got you," teased Jonathan. "Boy Tim, I didn't know you could run so fast!"

"Yeah, sign that boy up for the 100-meter dash," added Robert with a smile. "He's faster than a speeding bullet!"

With the light from Tim's flashlight, Grandpa and the cousins got four of their five flashlights working again. They examined the old mine car for a moment and then went to investigate what was behind the door. As they shined their lights through the doorway, they found a room about seven feet wide and ten feet long. There were several rudimentary shelves chiseled into the solid rock walls of the room.

"Here's what made all the racket," said Grandpa as he rolled a large timber out of the middle of the floor. "This beam must have been pushing on the back of the mine car and when we opened the door, it pushed the mine car out toward us."

Tim shined his light around the room. "It's empty," he said with disappointment. "Not even the shelves have anything on them."

"This probably used to be their explosives room," said Grandpa. "They probably kept their blasting powder and fuses on those shelves over there."

"But the lock," said Jonathan. "Why would they lock an old

mine car inside an empty room?"

"Maybe we should look at the mine car again," suggested Kimberly.

Grandpa and the cousins re-examined the mine car. "There's nothing unusual about this car," said Grandpa. "Cast-iron wheeled undercarriage, turntable, and a tilt-to-dump wooden box on it."

"But what about this?" said Lindy, pointing at the inside of the box. "There's something stuck here in this corner." Lindy retrieved her pocketknife and pried out the small object. "It looks like a chunk of gold!" she said excitedly.

CHAPTER 12

Haunting the Mine (Hi-Tech Style)

After a lengthy search had failed to uncover any further gold or clues, Grandpa and the cousins headed back down the hill to the ranch house. In her eagerness to show Grandma her discovery, Lindy ran ahead. She found Grandma Wright working in the kitchen.

"Well, what did you find?" asked Grandma.

Lindy held up her gold nugget. "This!" she said excitedly and handed it to her.

Grandma hefted the nugget in her hand. "It certainly feels heavy like gold," she said.

"And Tim was chased by a mine car monster," Kimberly announced as she entered the kitchen.

"What?" said Grandma. "Is he okay?"

The girls quickly told Grandma about their adventure as they washed their hands and joined in to help fix lunch. Grandpa and the boys put their locksmith tools away and joined them in the kitchen.

"Honey," asked Grandpa, "did the tow-truck get here yet to haul away the county car?"

"Yes, Bob McPherson's son, Mike, got here a little bit ago," Grandma replied.

"Good," said Grandpa. "I think I'll go see how he's doing."

"Well, take your sandwich with you so you don't get too hungry," Grandma suggested.

"Will do," Grandpa replied. "Thanks for the chow."

"Chow," chuckled Grandma to the two girls. "Sometimes he talks like he's still in the army."

"Can I go, too?" asked Robert.

"Sure," Grandpa replied. "Grab your sandwich and let's go."

When Grandpa and Robert got down to the tow-truck in the orchard, they found that Mike, the tow truck driver, had already loaded the crushed car and was strapping it down.

"Glad you suggested bringing a trailer," said Mike, cinching down his last nylon tie-down strap. "This car doesn't roll worth a bean."

Mike gathered up his tools and climbed into the cab of his truck. "Hey, that was something last night, wasn't it?" he said. "All those sirens!"

"What sirens?" asked Grandpa Charlie.

"You didn't hear?" said Mike with surprise in his voice. "The two kidnapper guys you caught out here broke free in Deputy Morrison's patrol car. They beat up Morrison and escaped into the woods near town."

"Thanks for the warning," said Grandpa. "We'll keep our guard up."

Mike started his truck and began to drive away.

"Say hi to your dad for me," Grandpa called out. "Oh, and Mike, on the car, send the bill to the county."

"Will do," said Mike with a smile.

"Wow," thought Robert. The idea of those two crooks on the loose sent Robert's mind racing.

When Robert and Grandpa got back to the house, Robert called a huddle and told the cousins about the kidnappers' escape.

"Boy," said Jonathan with concern. "The last thing we need is those two crooks coming back here again."

"And they will, too," Kimberly added. "Remember how they threatened Grandpa about coming back to get him?"

"*Nobody's* going to hurt our Grandpa," said Robert. "If those two creeps come back, they'll get more than they bargained for!"

"You mean we're going to set a trap for them?" said Tim with a growing, mischievous smile.

"Exactly," replied Robert with a grin. "And let's make it a doozie!"

It didn't take long for the cousins to figure out what the bait for their trap should be. A few minutes later, their grandparents received a phone call from a newspaper reporter in town. The reporter wanted to write a story about "Crazy Jake's lost gold mine being found."

Immediately after the phone call, a "Mr. O'Neal" from the county planning and environmental office called to set up an inspection appointment with Grandpa. Mr. O'Neal wanted to verify that Grandpa had the proper permits paid for—including a $25,000 permit fee for "storm water run-off"—to operate his newly discovered gold mine.

"Patience, Job, patience," reminded Grandma when Grandpa got off the phone.

The cousins continued their huddle. "How do you think they found out about Grandpa Jake's mine?" asked Lindy.

"The two crooks probably overheard Tim ask Deputy Morrison about 'picking the lock' in the mine," Kimberly replied.

"I didn't mean to—," Tim said defensively.

"What's done is done," said Jonathan. "We're just going to have to make the best of the situation. Now, if we're going to catch those guys, we'll need a few supplies."

"What's the plan?" asked Kimberly.

"Those crooks think there's a treasure in the mine, right?" said Jonathan. "Well, we'll just help them find *their* mine and, at the same time, give them the *scare* of their lives."

"Yeah," smiled Tim. "But instead of them hunting us, we'll *haunt* them."

Lindy giggled and said, "Tim, where do you get these awful jokes?"

"Sheer genius, I guess," Tim grinned back.

"Okay guys, we'd better get to work," said Jonathan, retrieving a pen and small note pad from a nearby desk. "We'll need some electronic supplies. Let's see, to do it right, we'll need some 2-way radios, a few lasers...."

Jonathan split the cousins into teams to get the supplies and the various "haunting" projects underway. That evening, the cousins reported their progress as Jonathan read down the checklist: "Infrared lights and sensors?"

"Purchased in town. Check."

"Motion sensors?"

"Check."

"Wireless audio speaker?"

"Check."

"Heavy fishing line?"

"Check."

"Super-bright starburst light?"

"Check."

"2-way radios?"

"Grandpa had some. Check."

"What's this?" said Jonathan as he studied the list. "12-volt car battery? 12-volt DC motor? Firecrackers? Toy rifle? Raccoon-skin cap? Halloween skeleton? I didn't put this on here!"

"Oh, that's *my* project," said Robert with a smile. "Tim and I are going to make a Bad-guy Chaser."

"Of course it'll have to be high-speed," Lindy teased.

"Of course," Robert grinned back. "But this time, I *might* include some brakes!"

CHAPTER 13

The Turkey Shoot

The cousins were awakened at 5:30 the next morning by a ringing phone. "Hello?" they overheard their grandmother say. "Yes, hi Sylvia. Yes, yes, he's here, let me get him. He's in the office." She covered the mouthpiece and called out. "Honey, it's Sylvia Martinez. Hurry!"

Grandpa's long-strided footsteps echoed down the wooden floor of the hallway.

"Hi Sylvia. What? Juan?! Where? Yes, we'll be right there!"

Grandpa hung up the phone. "Juan called Sylvia on their short-wave radio frequency. He's up near the 50-stamp mill. We've got to hurry before the kidnappers get back. She's calling the sheriff next."

The cousins scrambled out of their beds and hurried in to talk with their grandparents. Grandma gathered some emergency supplies. Lindy ducked into the kitchen and quickly re-emerged. "Here's an apple and some bread to eat on your way. We'll be praying for you."

"You kids hold down the fort," said Grandpa as he and Grandma hurried out to the ranch pickup and sped away.

Jonathan glanced at the rest of the cousins. "If we're going to hold down the fort, we'd better get moving. The sun's already up."

The cousins ate a quick breakfast and then Lindy, Tim,

Jonathan and Robert went up to the mine to finish their projects. Kimberly stayed at the ranch house to act as home base and warn the others by radio if someone arrived. She scanned the ranch with binoculars throughout the morning and was just about to stop for lunch when she caught sight of some cars coming up the long driveway. Excitedly, she keyed up her radio. "Jonathan, do you read me?"

"Roger," Jonathan's voice crackled back. "What's up?"

"We've got company. Two cars. One looks like a county car."

"How many riders?" asked Jonathan.

Kimberly re-focused her binoculars. "I count two men in the white county vehicle and three more in the second car."

"Identify them if you can. We don't want to bushwhack the wrong guys," returned Jonathan.

"Roger." Kimberly studied the men's faces in the approaching cars. "Two men from the ghost train and your angry crop duster. I don't recognize the other two. They're getting close to the house. They're getting out of their cars now and coming up to the front door." Kimberly backed into the hallway and whispered, "I'm *out* of here."

"Don't answer the door. Repeat, don't answer the door. Plan 'B' and stay on the line." Jonathan released the push-to-talk button on his radio and glanced across the ravine to where Tim was working at the spring tunnel entrance. He picked up a small rock and threw it in Tim's direction. The rock hit the door of the spring tunnel and ricocheted into the water. Tim thought the tunnel was caving-in on him and jumped backwards. He spied Jonathan trying to get his attention, recognized the signal, and got ready to set their decoy plan in action.

Cupping his hands around his mouth, Tim yelled at the top of his lungs, "**Robert! COME-UP-TO-THE-MINE!**"

The five men suddenly stopped on the front porch. "It's one of those kids," said the tall man from the ghost train. "Listen!"

"**Robert, come-up-to-the-mine!**" Tim yelled again, and then ran for the safety of their command post.

Mr. Stilt, the angry crop duster pilot, tried the doorknob. "The front door's locked," he said. "I say we go find Crazy Jake's mine and forget this other stuff."

Peering from a side window, Kimberly saw the five men leave the house and head up the hill. She clicked her radio onto transmit and whispered, "Coming your way, Jonathan."

"Roger," said Jonathan. "Battle stations, incoming enemy!"

Jonathan, Tim, Lindy, and Robert hunkered down in their dug-in command post across the ravine from the spring tunnel entrance.

"I think I see them coming," Lindy whispered a few moments later, peering through the brush and trees.

The five men paused for a minute at the cistern to look around, and then continued up the hill.

"It must be around here somewhere," said the tall man gruffly. "Keep looking." The group began to split up.

"We've got to keep them together," whispered Jonathan. "Tim, how's your throwing arm?"

"Good," said Tim.

"Try for the spring tunnel door," said Jonathan.

Tim, taking his baseball-pitching stance, wound up and threw a rock. It ricocheted off the door and bounced into the tunnel water with a loud *Splash!*

Mr. Stilt pointed in the direction of the spring tunnel. "The kids must be up there."

"Now we're getting somewhere," gloated one of the intruders, a bearded man in his late thirties.

With a smirk on his face, the tall man spied the spring tunnel entrance. "There's the mine. The kid must have gone in there," he said. "We'll take care of him shortly." He ordered his comrades to converge on the tunnel.

"Let's *inspect* this mine for the *county*," laughed the bearded man sarcastically.

"Keep it down," ordered the tall man. "Snake, you stand guard here in the doorway. And make sure we're *not* disturbed."

The man called "Snake" pulled out a pistol to stand watch while the other four men switched on their flashlights and climbed into the mine.

"So far, so good," whispered Lindy.

"Better switch on the infrared camera in the tunnel," directed Jonathan.

Robert switched on the power to the camera they'd borrowed from Mrs. Martinez. On a small monitor screen, the cousins could see the four men walking in the tunnel. The men disappeared for a moment as they explored the first two side tunnels and came back into view as they returned to the main tunnel.

"Is the mike system on yet?" asked Jonathan.

"It is now," replied Tim, switching on the power.

"Yech, I hate spider webs," said Mr. Stilt, trying to brush a large web from off of his face and chest. He got the synthetic web off, but the micro transmitter it had been carrying was now lodged on his shirt.

Jonathan grinned and said, "We now have audio."

"They're getting close to the "T" in the tracks," said Robert as he watched them on his split video screen. "Now, if they'll just all turn to the right and be the good creeps that they are..."

Inside the mine, the tall man barked his orders, "You two take the tunnel to the left; Stilt and I will go to the right. If you see anything, make sure *we* know about it."

"No, no, you turkeys," mumbled Robert, "you're not supposed to split up. You're all supposed to stick together."

The cousins watched nervously on their digital map of the mine as the crooks progressed.

The men in the right-hand tunnel were nearing the fifty-foot point. The men on the left were now at the forty-foot point.

"Come on, come on, go back to the *right*," urged Jonathan.

"The two men on the right are at the seventy-foot point," informed Robert. The cousins focused their full attention on the equipment before them. They weren't playing any video game this time; *this was for keeps.*

Robert tapped on his headphones and said, "Something's wrong with the microphones in the right tunnel. I'm not getting any sound."

The headphone speakers crackled with static as Jonathan wiggled the cable jack and Tim worked with the volume control knob. *Crackle-THWACK!*

Robert yanked the headphones off his ears. "Turn it down, turn it down!" he whispered. "It works *too* good now."

Robert cautiously put the headphones back on and listened. "They've found the ore chute in the right-hand tunnel. They think they've found something big. The tall man just called for the men in the other tunnel to join them."

"The two men on the left are heading over to the right-hand tunnel. Thank goodness," Lindy said.

"Whew," breathed Jonathan. "That was a close one."

Inside the mine, the arrogant tall man unlatched the small ore chute door. He was unpleasantly surprised as several large rocks tumbled out onto his toes. "Whoa-**OW!**" he said, angrily hopping around on one foot, holding his other foot in his hands.

"Thank you, thank you," whispered Tim, graciously bowing to the other cousins. "The rocks in the chute were my idea."

"Okay," said Robert, "let's give those creepazoids a really warm welcome."

The remote-control panel lit up with red and green lights as Robert switched on the power to his Bad-guy Chaser. Deep within the dark mine, at the very end of the tracks in the right-hand tunnel, Robert's machine began to hum.

Hearing the noise, the bearded man glanced down the dark tunnel. "What's that?"

"What's what?!" grumbled the tall man, still holding his sore foot.

"That humming sound."

"Aw, you're just hearing things," jeered the tall man.

"This place is kind of weird," complained the short man.

"Knock it off, you two," Mr. Stilt barked. "Now let's get looking for that treasure."

The two men reluctantly followed Mr. Stilt and the limping tall man down the tunnel past the ore chute.

"They're getting close," said Lindy as the cousins watched the men get to the ninety-foot point. "They're just about to enter the big room at the end of the tunnel."

"Tim, time to shed some *light* on the subject," whispered Jonathan.

"Ha-ha," replied Tim, pushing their "starburst light" button. The "starburst" light in the tunnel flared with blinding brightness, followed by a loud ***Ka-BOOM!***

"It's a cave-in!" shouted the bearded man, and the crooks dove for cover.

Hearing the loud rumble, Snake grew uneasy at the mine entrance. "What's going on in there?!" he called out.

"Hey, give us a hand," Tim replied over a speaker hidden twenty feet into the mine, imitating the tall man's voice.

Snake, taking the bait, hurriedly climbed into the mine in search of his companions.

Deep inside the mine, Mr. Stilt spotted Snake's flashlight creeping down the tunnel. "Somebody's coming," he warned the others.

"Freeze!" shouted the tall man, as he and Stilt blinded the intruder with their flashlight beams. Only then did they recognize their visitor. "Snake, what are you doing here?" the tall man asked.

"What do you mean *what am I doing here?!*" protested Snake. "*You're* the one who yelled for me to help you."

"No, I didn't," grumbled the tall man. "Boy, it's hard to get good help nowadays."

"You mean *bad* help," remarked an eerie voice from down toward the end of the tunnel.

"What was that?" asked the bearded man.

"What was what?!" Mr. Stilt barked back.

"I heard a voice down that away," complained the bearded man.

"Me too," piped in the short man.

"I didn't hear anything," spat the tall man angrily. "Now you guys knock off this wimpy stuff! Snake, you get back to the—."

Robert pushed another button on his remote control and his Bad-guy Chaser came to life. The men in the mine heard a mechanical rustle at the end of the tunnel and pointed their flashlights in its direction.

"It's just an old mine car," said Mr. Stilt as he spotted Robert's machine.

"*Just* a mine car, *phooey!*" replied a voice from within the mine car.

"Must be one of those brat kids," the tall man spat menacingly. "I'll silence him once and for all." He took a step toward the mine car to make good his threat but stopped when he heard a rattling-clanking sound coming from inside the car.

"I don't like it," complained the short man. "This place gives me the creeps."

Without warning, a skeleton wearing a raccoon-skin cap sat

upright in the mine car.

"A sk–skeleton! I told you this mine was haunted!" the bearded man stammered; his eyes wide as silver dollars.

"Howdy boys!" bellowed the skeleton as he raised a rifle to his shoulder and appeared to take aim. "Looks like we got us a turkey shoot. And if'n you boys aren't *the biggest turkeys I've ever seen.*"

"It's Crazy Jake!" whimpered the short man.

"Naw, it can't be," said Mr. Stilt, rubbing his eyes in disbelief.

The skeleton leveled his rifle. *KAPOW!*

"It's him!" yelled the short man as the five men hit the floor.

"Fire at him with your guns!" ordered the tall man.

"But it's a skeleton," replied Snake with a bewildered look on his face. "You can't kill skeletons, they're *already dead!*"

"I said, *fire!*" commanded the tall man.

BLAM! BLAM! The five men fired away at the skeleton. One of their bullets nicked the side of the raccoon-skin cap and spun it around on the skeleton's head.

"Shoot at me, will you!" called back the skeleton as he fired his rifle again. *KAPOW!*

Robert shifted another lever on his remote control. The mine car's 12-volt motor kicked into gear and started the mine car rolling toward the five men.

"It's coming after us!" shouted the bearded man.

The five men leapt to their feet and started backing away from the oncoming skeleton. They fired until their guns were empty, but the skeleton kept right on coming.

"Run for it!" shouted the tall man.

The five men turned tail and ran down the tunnel with the skeleton hot on their heels. The tall man glanced back and saw the haunted mine car right behind him. He threw down his empty gun and shoved his way past the other four fleeing men.

"Mess with my kin, will you?!" Robert's voice boomed through the skeleton's hidden speaker. "I'll show you. You boys are *history!*"

The five men, in their desperation to get away, ran straight on past the "T" as fast as their legs could carry them. Before they realized it, they were in the left tunnel. The tall man stumbled and fell, but his four partners only laughed, jumped over him, and kept right on going.

"I've got you now!" bellowed the skeleton.

With a loud shriek, the tall man leaped to his feet and ran like a wild man down the tunnel after the others. The five criminals dashed madly around the curve in the tunnel, plunged through the explosives room open doorway, and tripped over something invisible. They landed in a gasping, tangled heap against the back wall.

"The fishing line worked!" exclaimed Lindy.

"Yeeeee-hawwww!" shouted the skeleton in the raccoon-skin cap.

All five men looked frightfully down the tunnel as they saw the roaring mine car rounding the curve and coming toward them. The tall man shrieked, shoved Mr. Stilt off him, and desperately tried to climb up the solid rock wall behind them.

"The brakes," exclaimed Robert, reaching for a button that wasn't there. "I knew I forgot something. How am I going to stop the *Bad-guy Chaser?!*"

CHAPTER 14

The Door

"Close the explosives room door!" Jonathan yelled. "Close the door!"

Robert hit the last button. Just in time, a heavy weight swung down from the ceiling, slamming the strong door closed and locking it securely with a loud *Ker-THUNK!*

"We did it!" exclaimed Jonathan.

"Yeeeeeeeeeeeeeee-hawwwwwwwwwwwww!" shouted the cousins as they threw their hats into the air and whooped and cheered and danced for joy.

"Kimberly!" exclaimed Jonathan over the radio, "it worked! We've got them!"

"I know," Kimberly replied excitedly. "I could hear you guys all the way down here. I called the sheriff. *The troops are on their way!*"

Twenty minutes later, the cousins heard siren-blaring cars coming up the drive toward the house.

"Kimberly," radioed Jonathan. "Do you read me?"

"Loud and clear," Kimberly replied.

"When the deputies get there, bring them on up."

"Will do, big brother."

Robert, Tim, Lindy, and Jonathan walked over to the spring tunnel entrance to wait for the deputies. Lindy soon spotted Kimberly leading two deputies up the hill. "Here they come. It looks like one of them is Deputy Morrison."

Deputy Morrison introduced the cousins to his fellow officer, Deputy Garcia. The cousins quickly told the two officers about the situation in the mine and where the crooks were confined. "Great," said Deputy Morrison, "You kids wait outside the mine. We'll take over from here."

Switching on their flashlights, the deputies, guns in hand, climbed into the old mine. It seemed like an eternity to the cousins before they finally saw flashlight beams coming back toward them down the long, dark tunnel. Deputy Garcia led the five handcuffed crooks out of the tunnel, with Deputy Morrison bringing up the rear. As the cousins followed them, at a safe distance, down to the ranch house, they overheard the short man mumbling something about "never wanting to hear another word about skeletons, mine cars or lost treasure *ever, ever again*," and even the still-limping tall man seemed to agree.

The deputies crammed the crooks into their patrol cars and prepared to leave. "You kids did a great job in corralling these guys," called out Deputy Morrison with a smile and a wave. "And don't worry, this time we made *sure* they won't get away."

After the deputies had driven off, the cousins grabbed a quick bite to eat in the ranch house kitchen and headed back up to the mine to check on their "haunting" equipment. Jonathan, Kimberly, and Lindy worked on the command post while Tim and Robert went into the mine to retrieve the Bad-guy Chaser. After several minutes of searching, Tim and Robert emerged from the mine empty-handed.

"Hey guys," announced Tim, "we can't find the Bad-guy Chaser anywhere. It's totally disappeared."

"What?" said Kimberly, eyeing Tim with suspicion. "Tim, if this is another one of your tricks..."

"Honest," said Tim. "We looked all up and down the mine. We thought first that Deputy Morrison might have pushed it away somewhere. But we can't find the mine car, the skeleton, the rifle, or anything!"

"Tim isn't pulling your leg this time," Robert chipped-in. "We couldn't even find the raccoon skin hat!"

"Let's go have a look," said Jonathan a little skeptically. He led the cousins back into the mine. At the far end of the main tunnel, they turned left at the "T" and followed the tracks toward the explosives room.

"See what I mean," said Tim when they reached the room door, "it's gone."

"But mine cars don't just disappear," remarked Kimberly. "Maybe the crooks did something with it."

"I don't think so," said Jonathan. "Those guys were so dazed; they had a tough time even walking."

"Yes," added Lindy, "and they were all trapped in the explosives room until the deputies rounded them up. Robert, where was the Bad-guy Chaser when you lost control of it?"

"Well, it was chasing the crooks down this tunnel," replied Robert. "I remember seeing it entering the curve. I can't remember what happened after that."

"Then it must have gone off the curve somewhere," thought Jonathan aloud. "Let's see, the centrifugal force would have thrown it to the outside of the corner. Let's check the left sidewall for clues."

"I've got it!" said Tim. "*Maybe* the Bad-guy Chaser got lonely and went to visit the ghost train." The rest of the cousins just groaned and shook their heads.

"What are we looking for?" asked Kimberly as they examined the wooden-walled shoring in the curve.

"Scrapes, gouges, anything that might give us a clue about what happened to the mine car," answered Jonathan. Lindy, Kimberly, and Jonathan's search led them back toward the explosives room; Tim and Robert focused in the other direction.

"Let's see, if I were a skeleton in a mine car," said Tim, "where would *I* go?"

"That's easy," Robert smiled. "I'll show you. I'm an old pro at this mine car stuff!"

Robert walked fifty paces down the tunnel toward the "T", turned around, and ran back toward Tim as fast as he could go. "I've got you now, you creepazoids!" Robert shouted, pretending to be the Bad-guy Chaser in hot pursuit of the crooks.

Robert entered the curve at full speed, tripped on the track, and plowed into Tim like a football player making the meanest tackle of his life. Tim and Robert smacked into the wooden tunnel wall on the outside of the curve and, with a loud *THUNK*, disappeared into total darkness.

"I can't see a thing," whispered Robert a moment later, rubbing his eyes as he sat upright in the pitch-black chamber.

"*Now look what you've done*," gasped Tim. "You've gone and killed us both!"

"No I didn't," Robert replied. "I don't feel dead."

"I do," said Tim. "And besides, you're squishing me."

"You're not dead, then, because spirits can't feel," said Robert, feeling around in the darkness. "Now, where'd my flashlight go?"

Tim felt one on the floor beside him. "I found mine. Robert, would you *please* get off of me."

"I'm not on you, Tim."

"Well, if you're not squishing me," said Tim, his voice growing worried, "then who is?"

Tim lay as still as he could as he fumbled to find the switch on his flashlight. He hoped that by lying still and playing dead, *whatever* it was that was on him might go away. He turned his head slightly and a furry paw brushed across his chin. "Help!"

exclaimed Tim, switching on his light. He was face-to-face with a—a—a *raccoon skin capped skeleton?*

Robert burst out laughing. "Congratulations, Tim, you found the Bad-guy Chaser!"

Tim sat up, breathed a sigh of relief, and said, "Next time I go exploring *anywhere*, I'm going to tie my flashlight to my wrist."

Robert located his flashlight, too, got it working again, and then the two boys glanced around at their situation. Robert's fake skeleton lay at Tim's feet and the Bad-guy Chaser mine car was tipped on its side a few feet away. They were in what seemed to be an old secret passageway. They couldn't see the end of it.

"Before we do any more exploring," Robert gulped, "I vote that we get the others."

"Sounds good to me," said Tim. "Only one question. Which way is out?"

Robert looked puzzled for a moment. "Let's check for footprints," he said.

Retracing their tracks, they came to a wall. In the wall was a cleverly-hidden secret door, but no latch was apparent. After several attempts at trying to open the door, they began to grow more frantic. "Help! Help! Hey guys, get us out of here!" they pounded and shouted.

"Do you hear something?" Kimberly asked the others near the explosives room.

"It sounded like Tim," said Lindy.

"Listen, there it goes again," Kimberly said. "You don't really think this place is haunted, do you?"

"Don't be silly," said Lindy.

The faint voice soon stopped, followed by a thumping noise. Intrigued, Kimberly, Lindy, and Jonathan followed the pounding sound to its source. By the time they reached the bend in the tunnel, the banging had stopped.

"Tim, Tim, can you hear us?" called out Kimberly. "Where are you?"

"In here," returned Tim's muffled voice. "Push on the wall!"

"There's a secret door," Robert added. "We can't get it open."

Jonathan, Kimberly, and Lindy soon traced the outlines of the cleverly hidden door, but with the three of them pushing from the outside, and Robert and Tim pulling on the inside, the cousins still couldn't get the door open.

"This is crazy," said Jonathan. "There must be some way to open it."

The cousins stopped trying to force the door and instead started looking for a latch. Lindy discovered a small, rusty metal lever. At first it just looked like a part of the shoring, but when she twisted it, the secret door creaked open.

"Boy, are we glad to see you," said Robert, peeking his head out of the new opening.

"You should see the tunnel we found," said Tim excitedly.

"Really?" said Jonathan, starting to enter the new tunnel.

"Wait a minute," said Kimberly, "before we go in there, let's prop this door open so we can get back out."

"Good idea," said Jonathan.

Robert and Tim rolled the Bad-guy Chaser over against the door and wedged it in place. With the door now held securely open, Lindy, Jonathan, and Kimberly ducked through the doorway to join Tim and Robert. The secret tunnel was six-and-a-half feet tall and four feet wide.

"Look," Robert pointed out as they explored the old tunnel. "You can still see some pick marks in the ceiling and walls."

"Kind of gives you a funny feeling, doesn't it," said Kimberly. "Great-great Grandpa Jake might have been the last person to walk down this tunnel."

A glint of iron caught Jonathan's eye as he shined his flashlight down the passage. There, five feet above the floor, stuck into the right-hand wall, was an iron spike-like object. "Look at that," he said.

"What is it?" asked Kimberly.

"It's a miner's candle holder," said Jonathan as they stopped to look at it. "And look, there's still part of a candle in it."

Thirty feet further down the tunnel, they found another candle holder driven into the wall. At the end of the tunnel the cousins spotted a stack of wooden barrels.

"Maybe the gold is in those barrels," said Robert.

"There's one way to find out," said Jonathan. "Give me a hand."

Jonathan and Robert anxiously lifted down one of the top barrels and pried open the end. It was empty! They lifted down a second barrel and found it empty, too.

"Why would anybody hide a bunch of empty barrels?!" said Kimberly.

"Maybe this was their food storage room and these barrels held their dehydrated water," quipped Tim.

"Dehydrated water?" asked Kimberly.

"Yes," Tim said, "to use it, you just add water!"

"I'd like to add water to you," said Kimberly, reaching menacingly for her canteen.

"Hey, wait a minute," Lindy said excitedly, "there's another stack of barrels behind these!"

Working as a team, the cousins quickly removed the first wall of barrels, setting them along the left-hand wall, and started on the second stack.

"Boy, these barrels are a lot heavier," said Jonathan as he and Robert struggled to get down the first barrel from the new stack.

"Just think," quipped Tim, "if these barrels had jokes in

them, we'd really have a 'barrel of laughs'."

"Tim, I think you have been *cooped-up* for too long," Jonathan jested back.

The barrel slipped and went crashing to the floor, breaking open. A stream of glistening rocks poured from the barrel.

"Gold!" exclaimed Tim. "We found the treasure!"

Lindy reached down and retrieved some of the sparkling rocks. She studied the rock for a moment under the light of their flashlights. She dug out her pocketknife and tried scratching the rock. "I'm afraid it's just *fool's gold*," she said, finally looking up. "See how it flakes off when you pry at it."

Disappointed, the cousins returned to moving the wall of barrels. Lindy, always eager to add to her rock collection, dug down into the barrel, pulled out an especially pretty rock, and put it into her pocket to look at later.

As Robert and Jonathan lifted down another of the heavy barrels, Robert noticed something strange about the tunnel. "Hey guys, there's no wall behind these barrels," he said.

"You're right," exclaimed Lindy, shining her light. "The tunnel keeps on going!"

The cousins slipped past the barrels and into the tunnel beyond. After walking for twenty feet more, they came to a small, dark room. It was eight feet wide and fifteen feet long, with shelves set into each of the walls, but these shelves weren't empty!

CHAPTER 15

The Find

"Wow!" said Tim.

"Double wow!" smiled Robert as he spied two U.S. cavalry Sharp's rifles and some muskets leaning against the far wall. "And there's some pouches like the one we found at Lookout Point."

"Maybe there's gold in them, too!" exclaimed Tim as he and Robert raced across the room.

Robert quickly opened one of the pouches and dumped its contents out onto a shelf. "Rats," he said, "they're just full of *lead* bullets."

"Here's a box of candles," announced Lindy.

"Make that two boxes," added Kimberly from the other side of the room.

"Hey, look at this," said Tim, "I found some canteens and a bugle. They look just like the ones in my *Old West Cavalry* book back home!"

"Grandpa Jake had a bugle?" said Robert. "Do you think he's the one that rescued the people at Lookout Point?"

"Hey, does anybody know what *hardtack* is?" Kimberly called out from across the room.

Lindy glanced over her shoulder. "I think it's some kind of biscuit. Why?"

"I just found a box of it." Kimberly pried the box open.

"Oooo, yum-yummmmm."

"Do you think it might be a little stale?" asked Lindy.

"Just a little," said Kimberly, quickly closing the box.

"Speaking of food," said Robert. "Did anyone bring any snacks?"

Lindy picked up an old glass jar filled with slimy black stuff. "Here, have some of these *great* preserves, they're *only* a hundred years old."

"Ugh, I think I'll pass," said Robert. "I'm a little too young to die."

The cousins looked the room over from top-to-bottom and were just about to leave when Lindy noticed something in the corner. "Robert, look at this."

Lindy held up an old, dust-covered wooden chest. The chest was 9 inches wide, 18 inches long, 6 inches tall. Two leather straps were cinched around it to keep it closed. The straps broke as Lindy and Robert tried to unbuckle them. Inside the chest, they found a sealed, watertight tin box.

"Boy, what we need is a can-opener," said Lindy. "Robert, do you have your multitool knife?"

"Yes, but I don't think it works on this kind of thing," Robert answered.

"Let's take it down to the house," suggested Lindy. "If Grandpa's back, he'll be able to get it open."

"Good idea," Robert agreed. "Let's go."

The cousins collected some of the things they had discovered and headed down to the house "loaded for bear." On the way out of the secret tunnel, Robert jovially stopped at the fake skeleton. "Pardon me, old man," he said to the skeleton. "Do you mind if I borrow your coonskin hat?"

"Not at all, good fellow," the skeleton replied.

Robert squealed and ran out of the mine after the others. For some reason, Tim couldn't stop laughing all the way down to the house.

Grandma and Grandpa Wright were home.

"Captain Tim reporting for duty!" saluted Tim as he and all the rest of the cousins all filed into the living room to greet their grandparents.

Robert snapped to attention with his cavalry rifle. He had several leather pouches draped over his shoulders. "Sergeant Robert here too, sir!" he added with a big grin.

"Where on earth did you get those?" asked Grandpa.

"We found a secret room in Grandpa Jake's mine," Tim answered excitedly. "And it's full of all kinds of neat stuff!"

"And we found this chest, too," added Lindy. "It has a sealed metal box in it."

"Yes, Grandpa, we thought you could get it open," said Robert.

"*I'll take that!*" bellowed a threatening voice from the back porch. The cousins turned to see a dark-haired man, armed with a pistol, step into the room. "*Everybody get your hands up!*" ordered the intruder. "I came to *inspect* your lost mine, but it looks like you've already found the treasure for me."

"Who are you?!" challenged Tim.

"It's our *dear* Mr. O'Neal from the county environmental office," answered Grandpa with frustration. "He's the 'black widow' and 'thistle' guy."

"No one seems to *appreciate* my laws," replied O'Neal with an evil smile. "But you needn't worry; you won't be around long enough to be affected by them. You know, it would have been *so* much easier if you'd just knuckled under like the other ranchers.,"

"You'll never get away with this," said Jonathan defiantly. "We've already trapped your stooges!"

"Oh, please," said Mr. O'Neal, "Stilt and the others were just clumsy fools I used to help clear *my* beautiful mountain

THE TREASURE OF THE LOST MINE

park land. They just outlived their usefulness, that's all."

"The mine is on our grandparents' property," defended Jonathan. "You can't take it."

"Not anymore," boasted O'Neal. "This morning, I declared myself the sole *guardian and protector* of this whole mountain range. And, as my first official act, I've decreed that you *polluters* are to *disappear* inside Crazy Jake's lost gold mine...**forever!**"

"You can't kill us," countered Tim. "It's against the law!"

"Just pick up the things you brought down from the mine and carry them—very carefully—out to my car," ordered Mr. O'Neal.

"Take the treasure," said Grandpa Charlie. "Just leave my family alone!"

O'Neal glared in haughty defiance. "You had your chance to leave when I passed the environmental regulations, but you chose to fight me instead. I'll show you what happens to people who question the system. *Now get moving!*"

The cousins reluctantly picked up their treasure and began walking toward the front door. O'Neal followed them closely with his pistol aimed at Grandpa. "You punks try anything, and your grandpa and grandma won't even make it out the door."

"Drop it, O'Neal!" commanded a voice from the front entry.

"Morrison!" exclaimed Tim.

Everyone hit the floor as O'Neal swung to shoot the deputy. *KAPOW!*

O'Neal's shot went wide, hitting the wall beside the deputy and blowing wood splinters into the air.

Deputy Morrison returned fire and shot the gun out of O'Neal's hand. Like a scared animal, O'Neal turned and bolted for the back door.

"Take that!" yelled Jonathan as he threw the wooden chest at O'Neal, knocking him to the floor. "Everybody *dog pile!*"

The cousins leaped onto the fleeing crook. O'Neal flailed

about angrily, shook the cousins off, and was just about to get away when he ran into Grandpa.

"Don't mess with my family ever again!" shouted Grandpa.

Grandpa punched O'Neal in the jaw and sent him staggering backwards.

Deputy Morrison dove for the stunned O'Neal and knocked him flat. In a flash, Morrison had handcuffed the crook and searched him for more weapons.

"Nice guy," said Deputy Morrison sarcastically as he removed a hidden fighting knife from O'Neal's boot. Looking up, the deputy noticed the amazed looks on the cousins' faces and explained, "I used to rope cattle in the rodeo. You have to be pretty fast to catch those critters, too!"

As Deputy Morrison read O'Neal his rights, the crooked county administrator quickly regained his arrogance. "You've got nothing on me, Morrison," gloated O'Neal, rubbing his sore jaw. "I'm required by the county Environmental Protection Council to evict these *terrible* people. They got violent on me and I was forced to defend myself."

"Come on, O'Neal, you'll have to do better than that," said Deputy Morrison, shaking his head in disgust. "Let's see, there's trespassing, assault with a deadly weapon, kidnapping, willful destruction of private property, unlawful use of a controlled herbicide, fraud, attempted murder, and a few dozen more pages of charges."

O'Neal's face grew livid with anger. "These people have no right encumbering this land, it's *my* land."

"Fine, you can tell that to the judge. I'd say you'll have at least 50 or 60 years in prison to think about it. Last I heard, we still have some property rights in this country."

As Deputy Morrison led O'Neal out of the house, O'Neal cast a threatening glance at the cousins and their grandparents. "Knock it off, O'Neal!" ordered the deputy. "Now get into the car."

After securing O'Neal in the back seat of his patrol car, Deputy Morrison returned to the front of the house to discuss the case with the cousins and their grandparents. "I was afraid O'Neal would get desperate and try something crazy when you guys caught his henchmen," explained the deputy. "We've had him and his thugs under investigation for some time now."

"Well, thank you, deputy," said Grandpa Charlie. "You got here just in the nick of time."

"All in a day's work," smiled Deputy Morrison. "Hopefully, now that we've got O'Neal and his men behind bars, things will start settling back down around here."

"I can go for that," Grandpa agreed.

"So can we," remarked the cousins in unison. They all waved good-bye as Deputy Morrison backed his car out of the driveway and drove away.

"The box!" Jonathan remembered suddenly.

Grandpa retrieved some tools from the garage and, with Grandma and the cousins eagerly looking on, he quickly cut open the sealed tin box. When he peeled back the metal, he found an ancient-looking, leather-bound book.

"All that work for a book?" remarked Tim with disappointment.

Grandpa carefully lifted out the book. "Don't judge a book by its cover, son," he said.

Grandpa carefully opened the book, its pages old and yellowed. The pages were filled with beautifully handwritten, quill pen and ink words.

"It's my grandfather's journal!" said Grandpa, carefully thumbing through the pages. "Look, it tells about some of our ancestors and why they came to America."

Kimberly excitedly pointed at an object stuck between two pages. "Wait a minute," she said, "that looks like a photograph!"

Grandpa retrieved the photo and studied it for a moment. A smile came over his face. "This," he said, "is a picture of your great-great-grandpa and grandma and three of their children."

A few pages later, they found a second picture. "And here's Grandpa Jake and his wife again, older," noted Grandpa, "holding one of their grandchildren." Grandpa looked closely at the picture and smiled.

Who's the little baby?" asked Lindy.

"I'm not sure," Grandpa replied.

"May I please see the picture?" said Lindy. Grandpa handed it to her. Lindy studied it carefully and then turned it over. On the back of the picture were written the names Jake, Elisabeth, and Little Mudface.

"Little Mudface?" asked Lindy. "Who's that?"

"Little Mudface?" echoed Grandpa, blushing slightly. "Why, I haven't heard that name for a long, long time."

"But who is it?" Lindy asked again.

"Well," chuckled Grandpa. "It's me!"

"Little Mudface?" laughed Tim and the other cousins.

"When I was little," Grandpa explained with a big smile, "we'd go and visit my grandparents. I guess I always loved playing in the dirt and so Grandpa Jake called me his 'Little Mudface'."

"Well, it's time to get washed up for dinner, my 'Little Mudface', I mean, Honey," kidded Grandma lovingly. "We've got guests coming."

"Who is it?" asked Robert.

"Sylvia and Juan Martinez," Grandma replied. She smiled and held up her hand in anticipation of the cousins' questions. "Yes, he's fine, and yes, he can tell you all about his kidnapping and escape. Now, hurry and go get washed up for dinner."

"Grandma, what's for dinner?" called out Tim as he and the

other cousins washed their hands. "Steak, potatoes, and gravy?"

"No, *pizza*," answered Grandma.

"Pizza?" said Robert. "All right!"

"Hope there are at least five pizzas," Jonathan said with a grin. "Because I can eat a whole pizza all by myself."

When Sylvia and Juan Martinez arrived, they all sat down to eat. After the blessing on the food, the cousins asked Juan Martinez about his abduction.

"I've always been a railroad buff," Juan Martinez explained. "A few weeks ago, I caught sight of an old locomotive running on the logging tracks that somehow looked familiar to me. When I got home, I searched my train file and found an old newspaper clipping that I'd saved. It was a locomotive that had been bought at an auction a few years ago by a Mr. Frank O'Neal."

"We know him all too well," said Jonathan.

"But what would O'Neal want with an old train?" asked Robert.

"I had the same question," Juan replied. "A number of years ago, a new process was discovered that made it possible to get more of the gold out of gold ore. Groups went around re-processing all the old gold mine tailings. But somehow, the mines around here were overlooked. That was, until O'Neal came along. He and his gang were using the train on the old logging tracks to haul rock from the tailings of the mines in Coldwater Canyon. When I figured out what was going on, I contacted Deputy Morrison and told him all about it. I had arranged to meet him at the 50-stamp mill. I arrived at the mill a little early. Someone hit me from behind, and the next thing I knew, I was trussed up like a chicken in an old mine tunnel."

"Then the newspaper note we found on your desk was your appointment with the deputy?" asked Jonathan.

"Yes," said Mr. Martinez. "But deputy Morrison was delayed

in town and couldn't make it."

"How did you escape?" asked Lindy.

"I overheard my captors, a guy called 'Snake', and another man, talking about a lost gold mine that had been discovered. They couldn't stand being left out of the action and left me behind to go find it. I was able to get one of my hands free enough to untie myself. I located one of their radios and scrambled out of the mine to contact my wife."

"And I called your grandparents," said Sylvia. "They met me, and we all raced over and picked him up."

"But why all the secrecy about the train?" asked Kimberly.

"Simple," answered Mr. Martinez. "O'Neal and his gang were stealing the mine tailings from BLM land. It *wasn't* their land and it *wasn't* their gold."

"Mr. Martinez, there's something I've been wondering about," said Tim. "How did they make their ghost train disappear?"

"Good question," Mr. Martinez replied. "When I escaped, I found that the mine tunnel I had been held captive in went clear through the mountain behind the 50-stamp mill. You'd never know it. It was dug by the original miners in the Gold Rush days. At the mill's base, by Coldwater Stream, I also found a hidden turntable. The turntable was new. It was built by O'Neal and his gang."

"We never saw that," said Robert. "How did the turntable work?"

"When O'Neal's train approached Coldwater Stream," said Mr. Martinez, "the heavy weight of the locomotive triggered a switch and the turntable track swung out to bridge the stream where the tracks were missing. Once the train had crossed over the stream and entered the hidden mine tunnel, the track swung back. From there, the train traveled through the mountain to a quarry on the other side. At the quarry, O'Neal's gang used county trucks to haul the ore to another town to be processed."

"Whew," said Tim, "it makes me dizzy just thinking about it."

"Their plan worked great," continued Mr. Martinez, "until somebody wrecked their train. You should have seen it. The locomotive had slammed through a secret door at the end of the tunnel and landed upside-down on top of one of the county's dump trucks. It looked like the brakes must have failed."

The cousins all looked at Robert. "Hey guys, give me a *brake*," Robert said.

"Do you remember Mr. Stilt?" Grandpa Charlie asked the cousins.

"The 'angry crop duster'?" replied Jonathan. "Do we ever!"

"He was in cahoots with O'Neal," said Grandpa. "Mr. Stilt would offer to crop dust people's land for free, supposedly to gain business, and then he would spray poison from his airplane to kill the landowner's crops. Later, he would fly back over to re-seed the devastated fields with thistle plants. Once the thistle plants were growing, Stilt would notify O'Neal and they would condemn the land in the name of the county."

"I bet they sabotaged Jeb Carter's plane, too," said Robert.

"Right again," said Grandpa. "They didn't like his competition. Deputy Morrison said there will be a full investigation into all their criminal dealings, including the way O'Neal and his cohorts abused power—the outrageous permit fees and everything else—in the name of the county. We're organizing an oversight group to make sure the county stops illegally attacking us farmers and ranchers."

"Well, I for one am very glad those crooks, including O'Neal, are finally in jail," said Grandma.

"So are we!" said the Wright cousins in agreement.

"Grandma," said Grandpa with a wink, "how about some of your great dessert?"

"Coming right up," replied Grandma with a smile. The cousins' eyes lit up moments later as Grandma brought out bowls of fresh-baked, hot apple pie topped with big scoops of homemade vanilla ice cream and handed them around.

"Wow," said Robert.

"All right," relished Jonathan as he lifted up a spoonful of pie and said, "Grandma, *you're awesome!*"

CHAPTER 16

The Real Gold

The next morning, the cousins were up bright and early. They showed their grandpa the secret room in the mine and helped carry many of the old artifacts down to the house. Grandma was continually amazed as they stockpiled the articles in the living room and the dining room. Grandpa Jake's mine had finally been found!

"And Grandma," Tim said eagerly, "we found twenty-six leather pouches, just like the one at Lookout Point."

"Yeah, except these just have lead bullets in them," said Robert as he dumped the contents of one of the pouches out onto the sturdy dining room table. "See, they're—."

Robert's eyes were wide with surprise as two dozen round, *golden balls* rolled out onto the table. "

"But we checked. They were lead bullets up at the mine!" said Tim.

All the cousins joined in to dump the rest of the pouches out onto the strong wooden table. One of the pouches held lead bullets and all the others held gold.

Everyone picked up a gold ball to heft it for themselves.

"Wow," said Robert excitedly. "It's okay with me if they're not lead!"

"Gold bullets?" asked Kimberly.

"Before the attack," replied Grandpa, "the settlers must have been short on lead. In desperation, Jake must have made golden bullets as a reserve."

"Grandpa, would gold bullets really work?" asked Jonathan.

Grandpa Wright examined one of the bullets closely. "I don't know. I'd sure hate to waste any to find out, though."

"How much are each of these gold bullets worth?" asked Lindy.

Grandpa hefted one and thought for a moment. "Probably around $5,000 each," he said.

"And if we multiply that by the number of gold bullets we've found," Robert chimed in, "that will give us the total amount."

The family quickly gathered up all the gold bullets and counted them.

"Yahoo," said Tim excitedly, "we're rich!"

"Now Tim," said Kimberly, "this gold really belongs to Grandma and Grandpa. We found it on their property."

Grandma interrupted, "Since you kids helped us find the gold, you'll get a share of this family treasure, too."

"Thank you, Grandma," said Tim. "Wow, we can buy a big boat, and an airplane, and a submarine, and a car, and a—wow, we can buy all kinds of things with this gold!"

"Hold on," said Grandpa with a smile. "First, we'll have to pay the taxes so we don't lose this ranch. In the meantime, you guys can help Grandma and I make a *Needs and Wants List* so we don't waste this treasure. We want to use it wisely. We're Wrights, and Wrights use knowledge, tools, and treasure to build and to lift. We'll make Grandpa Jake proud."

"Grandpa, I think you'll get to keep your new tractor after all," said Robert with a grin.

"I think you're right," Grandpa smiled in reply.

"Boy," said Tim. "Gold bullets, cavalry rifles, canteens, now that's what I call a real treasure."

"Those are all wonderful and interesting things," said

Grandpa, "but you know, of all the treasures you kids found, I think my grandpa's old pictures and journal are the greatest treasures of all. That, and all of you, our wonderful family that's here to help each other out when things get tough."

"Like they told us at Smith Ranch years ago," added Grandma, "'The real gold you find in life is your family.'"

"Family hug!" called out Kimberly, and all the cousins rushed over to Grandma and Grandpa to share a family squeeze.

Later in the day, Jonathan called the Wright cousins together for a quick huddle. "Hey guys," he said excitedly, "Robert and I were just working on the barn and we found it."

"Found what?" asked Lindy.

"The turret for Grandpa's tank," Jonathan replied. "It's buried in the scrap metal pile behind the barn. And Grandpa says that since he doesn't have to sell his new tractor anymore, that we cousins can have full use of the tank."

"A tank with a turret on it?" said Tim excitedly.

"Yep," said Robert, "we could mount a big water cannon in the turret and enter the annual town water fight next week. We'd beat them all for sure."

"But they use big water balloon launchers and fire trucks and things," said Kimberly with concern. "Wouldn't those wipe us out?"

"Kimberly-Kim-Kim-Kim," said Jonathan, "we've got a World War 2 army tank. It's made of steel. It has bullet proof periscopes. A high-pressure firehose would only clean off some of the sand and dust."

"I'm in," said Robert with a grin.

"Me too," agreed Tim

"Me three," said Lindy. "Hey, speaking of dust and sand, I just learned about a lost Spanish galleon treasure ship. It's buried in the desert somewhere south of here."

Tim's eyes lit up. "Did you say lost treasure ship? Jeepers! What are we waiting for? We have some summer left. *Let's go find it!*

Please write a review
Authors love hearing from their readers!

Please let Greg Smith know what you thought about *The Treasure of the Lost Mine* by leaving a short review on Amazon or your other preferred online store. If you are under age 13, please ask an adult to help you. Your review will help other people find this fun and exciting new adventure.

Thank you!

Top tip: be sure not to give away any of the story's secrets!

About the Author

Greg exploring the bottom of the mine shaft seen in the book video trailer for *The Treasure of the Lost Mine*. You can watch the video trailer for this book at the author's website, GregoryOSmith.com.

Gregory O. Smith loves life! All of Greg's books are family friendly. He grew up in a family of four boys that rode horses, explored Old West gold mining ghost towns, and got to help drive an army tank across the Southern California desert in search of a crashed airplane!

Hamburgers are his all-time favorite food! (Hold the tomatoes and pickles, please.) Boysenberry pie topped with homemade vanilla ice cream is a close second. His current hobby is detective-like family history research.

Greg and his wife have raised five children and he now enjoys playing with his wonderful grandkids. He has been a Junior High School teacher and lived to tell about it. He has also been a water well driller, game and toy manufacturer, army mule mechanic, gold miner, railroad engineer, and living history adventure tour guide. (Think: dressing up as a Pilgrim, General George Washington, a wily Redcoat, or a California Gold Rush miner. Way too much fun!)

Greg's design and engineering background enables him to build things people can enjoy such as obstacle courses, waterwheels and ride-on railroads. His books are also fun filled, technically accurate, and STEM—Science, Technology, Engineering, and Math–supportive. Now, if he could just figure out how Tim Wright keeps drawing on his brand new book covers.

Greg likes visiting with his readers and hearing about their favorite characters and events in the books. To see the fun video trailers for the books and learn about the latest Wright cousin adventures, please visit **GregoryOSmith.com** today!

The Wright Cousin Adventures —
Get the complete set!

1   **The Treasure of the Lost Mine**—Meet the five Wright cousins in their first big mystery together. I mean, what could be more fun than a treasure hunt with five crazy, daring, ingenious, funny and determined teenagers, right? The adventure grows as the cousins run headlong into vanishing trains, trap doors, haunted gold mines and surprises at every turn!

2 **Desert Jeepers**—The five Wright cousins are having a blast 4-wheeling in the desert as they look for a long-lost Spanish treasure ship. And who wouldn't? There's so much to see! Palm trees, hidden treasure, UFO's, vanishing stagecoaches, incredible hot sauce, missing pilots. Wait! What?!

3 **The Secret of the Lost City**—A mysterious map holds the key to the location of an ancient treasure city. When the Wright cousins set out on horseback to find it, they run headlong into

desert flash floods, treacherous passages, and formidable foes. Saddle up for thrilling discoveries and the cousins' wacky sense of humor in this grand Western adventure!

4 The Case of the Missing Princess—The Wright cousins are helping to restore a stone fort from the American Revolution. They expect hard work, but find more—secret passages, pirates, dangerous waterfalls, a new girl with a fondness for swordplay. Join the cousins as they try to unravel this puzzling new mystery!

5 Secret Agents Don't Like Broccoli—The spy world will never be the same! Teenage cousins Robert and Tim Wright accidentally become America's top two secret agents—the notorious KIMOSOGGY and TORONTO. Their mission: rescue the beautiful Princess Katrina Straunsee and the mysterious, all-important Straunsee attaché case. They must not fail, for the future of America is in their hands. Get set for top secret fun and adventure as the Wright cousins outsmart the entire spy world—we hope!

6 The Great Submarine Adventure—The five Wright cousins have a submarine and they know how to use it! But the deeper they go, the more mysterious Lake Pinecone becomes. Something is wrecking boats on the lake and it's downright scary. Will they find the secret before it's too late? It's "up periscope" and "man the torpedoes" as the fun-loving Wright cousins dive into this exciting new adventure!

7 Take to the Skies—The Wright cousins are using their World War 2 seaplane to solve a puzzling mystery, but someone keeps sabotaging their efforts. Then a sudden lightning storm moves in and the local mountains erupt into flames. The cousins must fly into action to rescue their friends. Will their seaplane hold together long enough to help them survive the raging forest fires? Join the Wright cousins in this thrilling new adventure!

8 The Wright Cousins Fly Again—Secret bases, missing airplanes, and an unsolved World War 2 mystery are keeping the Wright cousins busy. Then the cousins discover a secret lurking deep in Lake Pinecone that is far more dangerous than they ever expected. Will all their carefully made plans be wrecked? Will they survive? You'd better have a life preserver and parachute ready for this fun and exciting new adventure!

9 Reach for the Stars—3-2-1-Blastoff! The Wright cousins are out of this world and so is the fun. Join the cousins as they travel into space aboard the new Stellar Spaceplane. Enjoy zero gravity and the incredible views. But what about those space aliens Tim keeps seeing? The Wrights soon discover there really is something out there and it's really scary. The cousins must pull together—with help from family and friends back on earth—if they are to survive. It's what family and friendship is all about. Get ready for fun and adventure as the Wright cousins *REACH FOR THE STARS!*

10 The Sword of Sutherlee—These are dangerous times in the kingdom of Gütenberg. King Straunsee and his daughters have been made prisoners in their own castle. The five Wright cousins rush in to help. With secret passages and swords in hand, the cousins must scramble to rescue their friends and the kingdom. Can they do it? Find out in this fun and exciting new adventure!

11 The Secret of Trifid Castle—A redirected airline flight leads the Wright cousins back into adventure: mysterious luggage, racing rental cars, cool spy gear, secret bunkers, and menacing foes. Lives hang in the balance. Who can they trust? Join the

Wright cousins on a secret mission in this fun, daring, and exciting new adventure!

12 The Clue in the Missing Plane— A cold war is about to turn hot in the Kingdom of Gütenberg. Snowstorms, jagged mountains, enemy soldiers. Can the Wright cousins discover a top secret clue before they become prisoners? Dive in with the Wright cousins in this thrilling new adventure!

Additional Books by Gregory O. Smith

The Hat, George Washington, and Me!—When a mysterious package arrives in the mail with only a tricorn hat and a playset inside, fourteen-year-old Daniel, of course, tries on the hat. Now he's in for it because the hat won't come off! Daniel suddenly finds bullies at every turn, redcoats pounding on the school room door, and a patriot in his cereal box! It's modern-day Millford—a town that is not on the map—and time is running out. Will Daniel and his friend, Rebecca, solve the mystery of the hat before it's too late?

Rheebakken 2: Last Stand for Freedom—The fate of the Free World is at stake. Alpha Command super-pilot Eric Brown has already had one airplane shot-out from under him. He's in no mood to let it happen again. Join Eric Brown, King Straunsee, and stubborn Princess Allesandra as they fight to keep freedom alive. Can they do it? This fast-paced, exciting new adventure is enjoyed by children *and* adults alike!

Strength of the Mountains—Balloon camping? The morning arrives. The balloon is filled. An unexpected storm strikes. Matt, all alone, is swept off into the wilderness in an unfinished balloon. Totally lost, what will he find? How will he survive? Will he ever make it home again? It's an exciting story of wilderness survival and growing friendships. Join the adventure!

Get the complete set!

Please tell your family and friends about these fun and exciting new adventures so they can enjoy them too!

Printed in Great Britain
by Amazon